The Lovely Dark

ALSO BY MATTHEW FOX

The Sky Over Rebecca

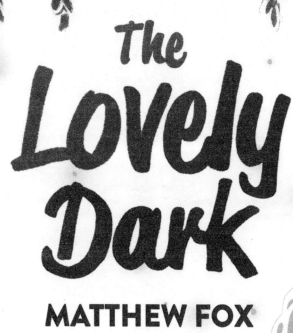

The Lovely Dark

MATTHEW FOX

HODDER

HODDER CHILDREN'S BOOKS

First published in Great Britain in 2023 by Hodder & Stoughton

1 3 5 7 9 10 8 6 4 2

A CIP catalogue record for this book
is available from the British Library.

ISBN 978 1 444 96474 5

Typeset in Horley by Avon DataSet Ltd, Alcester, Warwickshire

Printed and bound in Great Britain by Clays Ltd, Elcograf S.p.A.

The paper and board used in this book are made from
wood from responsible sources.

Hodder Children's Books
An imprint of Hachette Children's Group
Part of Hodder & Stoughton Limited
Carmelite House
50 Victoria Embankment
London EC4Y 0DZ

An Hachette UK Company
www.hachette.co.uk

www.hachettechildrens.co.uk

For Harry

Chapter One

It was raining the day my grandmother died. It was three years ago, in the first wave of the pandemic. We weren't allowed to see her in the hospital; we weren't allowed to visit. We weren't allowed to be with her at the end: nobody was, and she died alone.

There was a video link but she didn't want us to see her like that.

That day, all I could do was sit by the window in my room and look out on the rain and wait, and hope. I had a book open in my hands but I couldn't focus on the words; my mind wandered and I found myself staring at the toy boat on my windowsill. It was a plain wooden boat with a square of white sail and a little matchstick figure in the stern, and I imagined it outside in the rain; it was in the gutter, and a surge of rainwater carried it racing towards the drain in front of our house. There was nothing that could be done, nothing the matchstick figure could do about it: the storm was too strong. I saw the boat spinning in the swirl of water above the drain, and just as it disappeared through the gap between the bars, the phone rang downstairs, and I heard my dad answer it, and after a bit I heard him say, 'Thanks for letting us know,' and I knew that my grandmother had died.

She wasn't even particularly old, really; she was in her early sixties and full of beans, and by rights (so Dad said) she should have had another twenty years. I would have loved to have known her during those missing years: I could've used her advice, her help, her love, her no-nonsense approach. But it's the way things go.

My dad didn't cry that day – although he did later. He just went out for a walk and didn't come back for hours, and when he did come back he was wet through and cold to the bone, and it was still raining.

It rained the whole night and all the next day, and late in the evening I saw a ghost.

I was at my window again, with a book in my hands, and when I looked up from my book there was my grandmother, coming along the street: a thin woman, in a grey coat, holding a black umbrella, walking briskly towards our house. She came up the steps, glanced at her watch and rang the doorbell.

I closed my book and went downstairs. I was alone in the house; my mum and dad had gone to make the arrangements with the funeral director.

The doorbell rang again, and I opened the door. The wind gusted in and my grandmother stepped over the threshold, and shook her umbrella, and the rain came off it like spray from a wet dog. Then she turned and looked at me, and her eyes went wide with surprise, and her face went white.

'I'm early,' she said.

'But . . .' I said.

But you're dead, I was going to say.

'Forget I was here,' she said. 'I wasn't here, understand? I was never here.'

She was already on her way back out the door.

'But Grandma,' I said.

She looked at me. 'I love you, Eleanor,' she said, and then she closed the door, and I stood there in the darkened hall, breathing hard.

I realised I hadn't told her I loved her back.

I quickly opened the door to go after her, but there was

nobody there, only the wind and the rain, and when I looked up and down the road there was no sign of her.

No sign that she had ever been there.

I closed the door.

She was early, that's what she said.

Did that mean she was going to come back?

Chapter Two

What was so strange about Grandma coming back like that was that she didn't actually believe in ghosts. She didn't believe in anything. No God, no heaven, no reincarnation, nothing.

I was not sure what I believed, and Grandma didn't tell me what to believe either. She wanted me to make up my own mind – to believe in whatever I thought was true, so long as I was willing to stand up for it. We talked about these things many times in the years before she died. I practically lived at her house during half-terms or whenever I was off sick from school, and we talked about everything. We had conversations that lasted for days, it seemed: long meandering conversations about life, the universe and vegetarianism.

And we talked about Grandpa; he'd died two years before I was born.

'Where is he now, do you think?' I said, one day.

'Hm?' said Grandma; she was sorting through some clothes for a wash.

'Grandpa,' I said. 'Where is he now?'

'He's in Croydon cemetery,' she said.

'I know that,' I said. 'I mean the rest of him. I mean *him*.'

'I know what you meant,' she said, putting the washing in the machine.

'Where is he, then?'

'Nowhere,' she said, snapping the washing machine door shut. 'He's precisely nowhere. The particular arrangement of atoms and molecules that was him doesn't exist any more. There isn't any of him to be anywhere, if you see what I mean.'

'You don't think he's come back then?' I said.

'As what?'

'Somebody else,' I said. 'Another person on the planet.'

'No,' she said. She turned the washing machine on. Then she seemed to stop for a moment and think. 'But if reincarnation is true,' she said, 'I expect he's come back as a bumble bee. He loved his flowers.'

He did; the garden at the front of her house was still flourishing.

'What about you?' I said. 'What do you want to come back as?'

'I don't want to come back as anything,' she said. 'The end is the end, and I've accepted it as such. I have no fear of death. I imagine it will be exactly the same as it was before I was born. It won't feel like anything because I won't be there to feel it. I'll have no more awareness of it than a speck of dust floating in the darkness of space . . . It's quite comforting really, when you think of it.'

'But if you had to come back,' I said. 'As something.'

'If I had to,' she said, 'I suppose I'd like to come back as a tree. I'd like to live in a forest far away from people. I want to live for six hundred years and never have to meet a single human being.'

'Can I come and see you in the forest?' I said.

'No,' she said. 'Not allowed. Not until you're dead, anyway. Then you can also be a tree. We can grow side by side in the forest.'

'I'll be in your shadow,' I said.

She sighed like she was tired of all my questions. 'There's always something, isn't there, Eleanor?' she said. 'All right. Tell you what, I'll go and be something else first, and then we can both come back as a tree at the same time.'

'What will you be in the meantime?'

'A cactus,' she said. 'In a desert. Somewhere where there's no people, so I can get some peace and quiet. Somewhere I can get some thinking done.'

'OK,' I said.

*

Two days after the funeral, I bought a little cactus and took it down to Croydon cemetery and placed it on her stone. I looked for bumble bees in the flowerbeds between the graves but I didn't see any that day, and I wondered if they were together now, Grandma and Grandpa.

I didn't tell anybody about Grandma's ghost coming back.

I wasn't sure anyone would believe me anyway.

I held on to my secret. It was a promise.

She's going to come back. We're going to meet again.

Then a year passed, and she didn't come back.

And another.

Then almost all of another, and there was still no sign of her.

I spoke to her – when I was on my own – but she never

answered, which was a shame because I could have used her help on my homework; she'd taught history at a secondary modern in Croydon back in the day (as she used to say).

In the end I stopped expecting her to come back. I wasn't sure I'd really experienced what I thought I had: I wasn't sure I'd seen her ghost.

Maybe it was me; maybe it was all me.

I have been told I have what is known as an overactive imagination.

I do, but it's not my fault.

It's lockdown.

It's what happened to me during the pandemic.

The world outside shrank.

The world inside grew to fill the space that remained.

Chapter Three

The other thing that happened to me during the pandemic was Justin.

He moved into our street.

There was our house at the end of the road, and across the way was another house, exactly like ours, except that the other house had been empty for so long that there was a tree growing out of the roof. Nobody lived there: it was semi-derelict. There was knee-high grass in the small patch of lawn at the front and the bushes along the side had grown so tall and dense you could hardly see the house.

One day a sign went up.

FOR SALE.

People came to look at the house across the way; they

followed the estate agent inside in hard hats, and came out looking bewildered. Then another family came, and the dad went in by himself while the others waited outside by the car. It was a bright sunny day and I had gone back to my room to fetch another book (I'd been reading in the garden), and I stopped to look at the family outside. There was the mum, who was in her early forties, I think; she was very pregnant. There was the daughter, who was maybe seven or eight and who was sitting on the kerb reading a book, and then there was the boy, who was about my age, with glasses. He was standing a little away from the others making a paper aeroplane.

He looked intelligent. It wasn't the glasses he was wearing (he wasn't nerdy). It was more the focus he had, the concentration I could see on his face. Then he threw his arm back into the air and let the little aeroplane go . . .

It started well, gliding away, but then it seemed to change its mind. It turned back and spiralled downwards, and I watched (and the boy watched) as it dive-bombed into the drain in front of our house.

It vanished.

I laughed.

The boy looked up at me standing there in the window, and our eyes met.

He didn't seem to mind me laughing; he waved.

That was Justin.

Justin Fletcher.

His dad, Tony Fletcher, was an architect, and they bought the house two days later, and then they moved in, with a piano and everything, and Mr Fletcher set about doing the place up. It was a race against time, what with the new baby coming, and they lived by candlelight for a fortnight, cooking everything on a paraffin burner – although my mum and dad, being who they are, helped out: we put a wash on for them, and took over flasks filled with coffee, and kept their milk in our fridge, and their ice cream in our freezer.

Shortly afterwards Mrs Fletcher, whose name was Laura, came home from the hospital with the new baby (Daniel), and they were in.

They'd arrived.

Ayeesha was the girl, the middle child. She was eight. The piano was for her.

Justin was the boy. He was eleven going on twelve.

They'd moved from Greenwich.

He was going to go to my school.

Chapter Four

One bright, cold day a week later I went out on the rec with my kite. The wind was strong, and the kite kicked up into the air like a dog let off the lead. I let it play up there with its tail dancing happily below it, a red diamond in the sky.

The kite swooped and soared, and my mind emptied itself of all my worries.

The wind came harder and colder and tugged at my hands, and the kite whipped and struggled and jittered in the sky. Then the wind dropped – only for a moment, but it was enough – and the kite leaned over and sliced sideways down to the ground.

When I went to pick it up I saw Justin sitting on the bench by the entrance to the rec. He had a book in his hands and was wearing an orange cagoule that looked too thin for the weather.

I went over and said, 'Hi.'

'Hi,' he said.

'What are you doing?' I said.

He held up the book he'd been reading.

I nodded. 'I mean, what are you doing out here?'

Justin sighed. 'My sister is practising scales on the piano and my baby brother is screaming and the noise cancelling headphones I've ordered from Amazon aren't going to get here until Tuesday, so . . .'

'You could go to the library,' I said.

'The library smells,' he scowled. 'No, I'm fine here, thank you.'

He didn't look fine.

He looked like he needed a friend.

'What's the book?' I said.

He showed it to me: it was the new Philip Pullman. One I hadn't read yet.

'What's it like?' I said.

'It's magical and dark and serious,' said Justin. 'You can borrow it when I'm finished with it.'

*

Very quickly our books made us friends. Books are the key, you see. When you meet someone new and they've read the same books as you, or some of them anyway, and they feel the same way you do about them, it means they're all right in your book. It means you can understand each other. You have a kind of shared language.

Justin had read all the books I'd read and more. He was unstoppable: he knew way more stuff than me; he was cleverer than me, too. He wanted to be a teacher or an architect when he grew up, he said, and when he asked me what I wanted to do, I had to admit I had no idea. Except I knew I didn't want to be a teacher.

'Why not?' he said.

'My dad's a teacher,' I said. 'My grandma was a teacher.'

'So?'

'It seems unimaginative,' I said.

*

I didn't tell Justin about Grandma coming back.

About her saying she was early.

He didn't believe in ghosts, or heaven or hell, or anything spooky.

If I had told him, he would just have tried to find a

rational explanation for what I thought I'd experienced. He would just have said I was sad and upset at the time, and I was grieving, and I desperately wanted to see Grandma again, so I did.

He would have said I'd wished her into the world.

And maybe he would have been right.

Maybe.

Except . . .

Maybe things are more complicated than that.

I should probably tell you about the girl who looked like me.

Chapter Five

As we were leaving school one day Justin's phone lit up with notifications as soon as he turned it on: it buzzed and buzzed and buzzed until finally he stopped and looked at the screen.

It was starting to rain.

Justin stared at his phone; he didn't say anything for a moment.

'What is it?' I said.

'A girl at my old school,' he said. 'She got Covid.'

'Is she OK?'

He shook his head.

'Is she dead?' I said.

'She's in a coma,' he said.

'Is she asleep?'

'She's unconscious,' he said. 'It's the only way they could keep her alive.'

'. . . Is she gonna be all right?'

'They don't know,' he said. '. . . Her parents are asking people to pray for her.'

'Are you going to?'

Justin gave me a look that said *No*.

'I'm going to ask my mum to pray for her,' he said.

I nodded. 'I'm sorry,' I said.

'It's OK.'

I could see he wasn't OK.

The rain came on harder, and Justin took out his cagoule and held it above our heads, and we walked to the tube station. He didn't say anything else about the girl from his old school, and I wasn't sure if there was anything I could say to make him feel better. Inside, we went down the escalator to the westbound platform and got on the train, and it pulled away from the station. The lights flickered, like there was something wrong with the electrics, and then they went out. For a second, maybe two seconds, all I could see was the glow from people's phones, and when the lights came on again the train slowed, and came to a halt in the middle of the tunnel.

A voice over the tannoy said we were waiting here for a signal.

There was another sound, a screeching and a low engine sound, and another train appeared, going in the other direction, and stopped right alongside us.

We could see the people on the other train and they could see us.

'What was her name?' I said.

'Who?'

'The girl, at your old school.'

Justin wasn't looking at me; he was looking past me, at the other train.

'Her name was . . . Aisling,' he said. 'It's, um, Irish.'

He went back to staring at the people on the other train.

'Did you like her?' I said.

'Did I what?'

'Hey,' I said. I clicked my fingers in front of his face. 'Did you *like* her?'

Justin looked at me and pushed his glasses up his nose, and then he said, very slowly and calmly, 'Ellie, I need you to look at something.'

'Answer me. Did you like her?'

Justin ignored me. 'Turn around slowly,' he said, 'and look behind you.'

'. . . All right.'

I turned, and I didn't understand what I was looking at.

'That girl,' said Justin. 'She looks just like you.'

He was right. There was a girl on the other train who looked a lot like me. In fact, she looked so much like me that for a moment I thought I was looking at my reflection. But then the girl – over there, on the other train – would have been looking right back at me, and she wasn't. She was sitting facing the direction the other train was going in.

'Actually,' said Justin. 'She looks exactly like you.'

'She does,' I said.

She didn't just look *like* me. She looked *exactly* like me.

Her hair was the same as mine: the same colour, same cut.

Her face too, her skin.

I began to feel a little sick. It was a queasy, dizzy, spinning feeling.

It felt like I was falling.

'She has the same backpack as you,' said Justin. 'The jacket's the same too.'

Everything was the same.

'You could be twins,' said Justin.

Identical twins.

I was feeling very unwell.

Justin reached past me and knocked on the window.

'Don't,' I said quietly. 'Don't.'

Cold water ran through my insides. A hand seemed to grab my stomach.

'Hey!' said Justin, knocking on the window again.

The girl who looked like me didn't hear Justin knocking, although the passenger sitting opposite her looked up from his newspaper and frowned.

'Hey!' said Justin again.

The girl who looked like me kept staring straight ahead.

Justin knocked on the window again.

'Stop it,' I said. 'Please . . .'

Justin looked at me. 'Are you all right?' he said. 'You look a bit . . .'

'I have to get off this train,' I said, and stood up, and as soon as I was on my feet there was a jolt and a momentary blink of darkness, and then the train – our train – started moving, pulling away from the other train, and I saw the girl who looked like me glance at her watch, and then she was gone, and I had no idea what had happened and who she could possibly be, if not me.

A moment later I heard grandmother's voice in my head.

That, she said, *was a fetch*.

Chapter Six

'How are you feeling?' said Justin.

We were sitting on a metal bench at the far end of the platform. My head was between my knees; I'd been like that for about twenty minutes.

I hadn't actually been sick but I would like to have been; it might have made me feel a bit better.

'Here,' said Justin. 'Water.'

I brought my head up slowly and looked at him. He handed me a bottle of water he'd bought from a vending machine and I drank from it.

He'd helped me off the train, I remembered. Then he'd half pushed, half carried me to the bench.

I laid my arms across my knees and rested my head there for a bit.

22

*

The rain had eased off, but it was still drizzling a bit. We were walking back through the rec towards our road. The trees were bare with slicks of brown leaves on the ground.

I was feeling better, then worse, then better again, but I could walk.

'What's a fetch?' said Justin.

'What's that?' I said.

'You said something about a fetch. Back there, in the station.'

'Oh,' I said. I didn't remember saying anything about anything.

Justin looked at me.

'A fetch is a double,' I said.

'Ah,' said Justin.

'It's from Irish folklore,' I said. 'It's a premonition. A warning. It means your double has come from the world of the dead to fetch you. It means you're going to die . . . It means I'm going to die.'

'Except it doesn't mean anything of the kind,' said Justin.

I stopped. Justin stopped too.

'It's called a *doppelgänger* in German,' said Justin. 'It's a medieval superstition. It's just a scary story, like all the

23

other scary stories. Somebody made it up.'

'Maybe they made it up because it's true,' I said.

'That – I don't know what to say to that . . . You're not going to die.'

'You don't know that,' I said, walking on.

'No,' said Justin, 'I'm pretty sure I know that.'

'How come?'

'Because this is the twenty-first century. Because we have science and medicine and satellites. Because there's nothing wrong with you. You don't even have allergies.'

'I have allergies,' I said, stopping again.

He shook his head. 'You got scared,' he said. 'That's all.'

'You saw her,' I said. 'She looked exactly like me.'

'She did,' he said. 'But it doesn't mean anything. It's just chance. Think about it. There are a lot of people living on this planet right now – a *lot* of people, nearly eight billion of us – and some of us are going to look like each other. There are going to be people out there who look like me too, Ellie. And seriously, we have more important things to worry about than superstitions.'

He was probably right; we walked on a bit in the rain.

'Besides,' said Justin, 'she was wearing a watch.'

'Who?' I said.

'The girl on the train. Your double. She was wearing a watch.'

He was right. I remembered it now. She'd looked at her watch just as our train started pulling away. It was a silver one, old-fashioned, with a black strap.

'And you don't wear a watch,' said Justin.

I put my hand to my left wrist. I don't wear a watch; I just use my phone.

'So there's a difference between you and the girl on the train,' Justin said. 'If you're looking for a difference. If you need her *not to* be you, she's not you.'

He was always a step ahead of me.

'You're right,' I said. 'She's not exactly me.'

If there was a difference between us then the girl who looked like me wasn't my double, and if she wasn't my double she couldn't *fetch* me.

I wasn't going to die.

Justin's phone buzzed again.

The girl at his old school, I thought.

She's dead.

She's dead and I'm alive.

Immediately I felt bad for thinking it.

'What is it?' I said.

'Text from my mum,' he said. 'She wants me to pray for that girl.'

'You should do it,' I said.

He sighed. 'It can't help.'

'It can't hurt either,' I said, and we walked on in silence.

Chapter Seven

What I hadn't told Justin was that I had a watch, exactly like the one the girl on the train was wearing. It was my Grandma's watch; my parents had given it to me after she died. I wore it all the time until I got my new phone, and then one day I just forgot to put it on.

When I got home I went up to my room and pulled out a box from underneath the bed and opened it, and there were the things I'd inherited from Grandma: lots of her jewellery (in little cushioned boxes), a pair of gloves, an old scarf wrapped in soft tissue paper, an album of black and white photographs – and, somewhere here, her old watch. There was also my dad's Walkman, which had come from Grandma's house after she died (and which I'd had to rescue from a box destined for the charity shop):

it was blue, and the size of a book, and it still worked if you put batteries in it. I'd kept some of dad's tapes too – ones he'd recorded himself, with his teenage handwriting down the spines and on the labels inside.

Underneath his Walkman was Grandma's watch. It was silver and elegant, and it had a black strap.

It was the same watch the girl who looked like me had been wearing.

I was sure of it.

In which case . . .

I was going to die sometime soon.

Was that why Grandma had come back? To warn me?

I could ask her what was going to happen to me if she came back; she would probably know, being dead herself.

I looked at her old watch. The stopped hands on the analogue face made me feel guilty somehow. I held it up to my ear – the metal was cold – and then I turned the wheel and wound it up. It began to tick loudly in the quiet room, and I set the time, wondering just how long I had left to live and how, exactly, I was going to die.

Death was everywhere, really. Death could come from any direction.

I put Grandma's watch on the windowsill, next to the little wooden boat.

I wasn't going to tell Justin about this.

I wasn't going to tell anyone about this.

I would just have to be careful never to wear the watch.

I would just have to be careful about everything.

Chapter Eight

The next day – the very next morning, in fact – I woke up with a temperature.

Dad came in and put his hand on my forehead.

'I'm dying,' I said.

'You're not dying,' said Dad. He went downstairs and came back up again with the thermometer, which he stuck in my ear.

It beeped.

'Thirty-nine point six,' he said. 'Warm enough to stay off school.'

'That's good,' I said. 'I don't want to die at school.'

'You're not dying.'

He went downstairs and came back up with a Covid test kit.

'Sit up,' he said. He swabbed the back of my throat and then stuck the little stick up my nose. The plastic test panel lay on the windowsill next to grandmother's watch. I could hear it ticking; I watched the hands turn through fifteen minutes, then twenty, and then my dad came in again and leaned over me to look at the test.

'Negative,' he said.

Downstairs, Mum and Dad had also tested negative.

I had something else.

I had the flu.

*

My parents couldn't afford to take a day off work to look after me, so in the end it was left to Laura, Justin's mum, who was off with the baby, to pop across the road every couple of hours to check on me, to take my temperature and to remind me to drink lots of water.

She brought soup with her, and the baby. I ate the soup but not the baby, I think: I'm not sure; I wasn't really there. A little cactus, like the ones you get at Ikea, appeared on the windowsill. I told Mrs Fletcher the cactus was a message from my grandma: it meant everything was going to be all right; I wasn't going to die.

I reached out and pricked my finger on it and there was blood.

'You're hallucinating,' said Mrs Fletcher.

Then there was no one in the room and the cactus was gone. I looked at the watch, ticking steadily on the windowsill.

It was four o'clock in the afternoon.

Dad came in with a cup of tea and some eggs on toast on a tray.

He put his hand on my forehead and nodded.

The fever had broken.

'What day is it?' I said.

'It's Friday,' he said.

'I thought it was Tuesday,' I said.

'It was Tuesday,' he said. 'But now it's Friday.'

I drank the tea and ate everything on the plate and went straight back to sleep. There was a moment of darkness and then it was light again in my room, and the cup and the tray were gone, and the door opened and my dad came in quietly.

'Sleeping Beauty,' he said. 'Are you awake?'

'I'm alive,' I said.

'That's good,' said Dad. 'It's Saturday.'

He leaned over me and opened the curtains.

'We've got some news,' he said.

Chapter Nine

'How do you know it's a boy?' I said.

'They took a picture,' said Mum. 'She did. The nurse.'

'An ultrasound,' said Dad.

We were downstairs in the kitchen. I was still in my pyjamas. They'd just been up at the hospital. I remembered them saying something a while ago about Mum having to go for a routine appointment sometime soon. But there was nothing routine about it at all. It was a fourteen-week scan: my mum was pregnant.

I was going to have a baby brother.

When did they get so good at keeping secrets? I wondered, looking at them sitting across from me at the kitchen table. They could never keep anything secret before. But then I'd been distracted. I've been in a world of my own the whole three years of the pandemic.

'Here,' said Mum. She opened a plain brown envelope lying on the table between us and slid out some small black and white photographs. She handed one to me. 'This is for you,' she said.

I looked at the picture. It was on some kind of shiny paper and it didn't look like anything much. It was mostly black with some grey patches here and there. It looked like a satellite picture of the weather.

'This is an image from inside the womb,' said Dad, who was a science teacher at a school in another borough. He was about to go into one of his long rambling explanations of things. 'It's called an ultrasound because it uses sound waves to create an image—'

'Here's the head,' said Mum, cutting him off, pointing to a particular grey blob on the picture in front of me. 'Do you see?'

I saw it.

Yes.

Wow!

'And this is the rest of him.'

Yes!

'This is for you to keep,' said Mum. 'We took two copies. One for us, one for you.'

'We thought you'd like a picture of your baby brother,' said Dad.

I did. I stared at the picture and realised I was looking at the future.

My future, my little brother's future, our future.

The ultrasound was a window into another world, a dark and watery world, a world of two hearts beating and blood rushing everywhere all at once.

I wondered if he was dreaming in there.

Or just sleeping in the warm darkness.

My mind reeled, swirling with ideas about what it would be like to have a baby brother and how soon was the baby coming, and what he was going to look like, and who he was going to be, and I thought of my grandma and how she would've wanted to be here for this, and for some reason I saw her smiling.

'Are you pleased?' asked Mum.

'Yes,' I said. And then, 'What are you going to call him?'

'Not sure yet,' said Dad.

'We have some thoughts,' said Mum.

'You should call him Jack,' I said. I looked right at Dad. 'After your mother. She was Jackie, wasn't she? I mean . . .'

I stopped.

I hadn't meant anything by it.

I hadn't meant to upset him.

Tears shone in his eyes, and then the floodgates opened and tears ran down his cheeks, and he couldn't say anything for a while.

'Did I say the wrong thing?' I said.

'No,' said Mum, holding Dad's hand. 'No.'

Dad was smiling through his tears now.

'It's all right,' he said finally. 'It's all right . . . I'm happy.'

*

I went back to bed and slept some more. I'd put the ultrasound picture on the windowsill next to Grandmother's watch: it was still there when I woke up, which meant it wasn't a dream, and I was glad.

Chapter Ten

A terrible storm arrived on Monday morning and didn't go away until Wednesday. It was half-term – I was off school for a week and I'd recovered from the flu, but I was still stuck in the house.

The wind whipped up and down the street and the rain came in great sloshing waves all through the morning; there was no going out in it. I sat at my window with a book open in my lap and tried to read, but the storm was too fierce, too fascinating – too watchable. I saw a black umbrella flying through the air, spinning as it went. Leaves that had stayed on the ground in great soggy slicks since the autumn were ripped up and swirled around above the houses. The lamp post across the road swayed.

There was a *flash* of lightning two or three streets away

and then I heard a *clunk*, and the electricity went off.

For an hour or so, it was only our side of the street. The Fletchers across the road still had power and they boiled the kettle, and Justin brought us over a flask of coffee, and his mum set about making room in their freezer to rescue some things from ours. The pub at the end of the road, the Traveller's Return, still had power and we thought maybe we could go there for dinner, if we could face the rain.

Then there was another great gust of wind and the lights in the windows on the other side of the street went out, and so did the streetlights, and the pub went dark too.

*

Justin came across the road in the early evening and we camped out in the den upstairs and studied by candlelight, surrounded by cardboard moving boxes that had come from Grandma's house, and all of my dad's clutter: his desk, his record player and LPs, a pile of board games he'd had when he was a kid.

Justin was helping me catch up on the lessons I'd missed when I was off with the flu. It was a choice between maths, geography and history, he said. I chose history.

What I'd missed was the ancient Greeks and what they thought happened to you when you died. Justin opened my textbook for me and rifled through the pages until he found a drawing of a river and a boat tied up to a little jetty.

'There's a river,' said Justin. 'It separates this world, the world of the living, from the next world, the world of the dead. And there's a ferryman, a boatman, who'll take you across the river in his boat.'

He turned the pages of my textbook in the flickering candlelight.

'The river is the Styx,' he said. 'Styx. S – T – Y – X.'

I wrote it down in my exercise book.

'The boatman's name is Charon,' he said, and I wrote that down too.

'And the underworld is called Hades,' he said.

I wrote down the word Hades and stared at it.

'Like the word "shade",' I said.

'Exactly,' said Justin. 'Like "shade". Like "shadow".'

'A shadow world,' I said, and Justin nodded and turned the page again and found a picture of an old Greek coin with a strange grinning face on it.

'Now the weird-in-a-good-way thing about this trip is, it costs money. You need to pay the ferryman; you need a coin, called an obol. Because what the Greeks did was, when somebody died, they put an actual coin in the dead person's mouth so they'd have the fare to pay the ferryman.'

'What happens if you don't have any money on you?' I said.

'Not money,' said Justin. 'A coin. You can't pay with a debit card or your Oyster card or anything like that. You need an actual coin.'

'All right. What happens if you don't have a coin?'

'It's unclear,' he said. 'Some people think you roam the banks of the river for a hundred years. And some people think the ferryman just won't take you. You'll be stuck here in the land of the living forever.'

'A ghost?' I asked.

'A ghost,' said Justin.

Neither of us said anything for a moment. The candlelight flickered between us as if there was a draught somewhere, but all the windows were fastened tight against the storm. Justin reached for the flask of hot chocolate he'd made on his dad's paraffin stove. Then there was more lightning: two strikes far away across town and the room was as bright as day for a moment, then dark again.

Justin poured the last of the hot chocolate into our cups.

'Justin,' I said.

'Yes?'

'If I die – and I'm not saying I'm going to die anytime soon by the way.'

Justin sighed. 'Here we go again. You're not going to die,' he said.

'I know,' I said. 'I know that. But *if* I do, when I do, you're going to have to put a coin in my mouth.'

'Eleanor, you're not going to die.'

'No, listen,' I said. 'I'll do the same for you. I'll put a coin in your coffin.'

'How are you going to do that?' he said. He was almost smiling.

'I don't know,' I said. 'I'll find a way. I'll smuggle it in.'

'All right,' he said. 'What sort of coin?'

'Maybe a fifty-pence piece?' I said.

'A fifty-pence piece?'

'A pound then.'

He wasn't impressed.

'Two pounds then,' I said.

'Forget it,' he said. 'You're not going to die anyway.'

'Just say you'll do it.'

'I'm not going to do it,' he said. 'If we find out you're going to die, we'll figure out a way to stop it. I'll figure out a way to stop it.'

'Like, what?' I said. 'Like if I have a disease, you'll cure me?'

'Something like that.'

'You're not that clever,' I said.

'How do you know?'

'Nobody's that clever,' I said.

'People are clever,' he said. 'People cure diseases all the time.'

'I thought you wanted to be an architect, anyway. Not a doctor.'

'I'll do what I have to do,' he said gloomily.

'I still want a coin,' I said.

'I'm not doing it,' he said. 'I'm not going to put a coin in your mouth. I'm not even going to say I'm going to do it just to please you.'

'Why not?' I said.

'. . . It's bad luck,' he said.

Chapter Eleven

The storm raged into the night. There was an orange glow in the sky, which meant there was power somewhere in the city. But around where we lived, all was dark, and I lay in bed in an enveloping blackness.

I wasn't afraid of the dark – not now.

Once upon a time I was afraid of what might be hiding in the shadows by my bookshelves and in the dark behind the door, and I slept with the light on.

Then came the pandemic, and the first lockdown, and the world turned inside out.

The danger wasn't in here, in my room. The danger was out there, in the air, and leaving a light on in here made no difference: it had killed my grandmother anyway and from then on, I slept with the light off.

That night, while the storm came and went, I lay in bed listening to the water gurgling in the radiator by my bed, and I pretended I was hibernating, waiting for a faraway spring. There was something about the dark and how warm it was, and how safe I felt in here: I didn't ever want to get up; I wanted to sleep forever.

Let the storm rage on.

I'm here in the lovely dark.

Chapter Twelve

I'd missed a school trip to see a mosaic the week I'd been off sick, but Justin said I *had* to see it, and he wanted to see it again anyway, so the two of us went on Thursday.

It was a Roman mosaic: it had been discovered, just recently, at the deepest point on the London Underground. Some essential safety work was being done at London Bridge station and the work had revealed a mosaic, thirty metres below sea level, deep down in the earth. All the work had to stop while a team of archaeologists came in from one of the universities to study it and decide what to do with it. And until they decided what to do with it, they were letting schools in to see it, and ticketed visitors at other times.

'They think it's a shrine,' said Justin. We were on the

tube heading east across town. 'A temple. Dedicated to Orpheus. He wasn't actually a god, but he was kind of a key figure in Greek mythology. The pictures in the mosaic tell his story.'

'I thought you said it was Roman, this mosaic,' I said.

'It is,' said Justin. 'The Romans culturally appropriated all the Greek myths.'

'They culturally what?'

'They stole them,' he said. 'The Romans stole the Greek gods and renamed them. They took the stories too, including the one about Orpheus.'

'He's the god of dreams, right?'

'No, that's Morpheus. Orpheus is . . . something else. It's kind of a strange story.' He seemed perplexed. I watched his brown eyes behind his glasses. 'I don't know how I feel about it,' he said finally. 'I'm not even really sure I understand it.'

The train pulled into London Bridge station.

'This is us,' he said and we got to our feet.

As we stepped off the train someone brushed past me, and for a moment I thought I saw Justin getting back on the train.

Except it wasn't him; it couldn't be him. Justin was over

there putting some coins into a vending machine.

I watched the boy who looked like Justin move through the train carriage and find a place to sit down.

They're the same, I thought. *They're exactly the same: the orange cagoule, the glasses, the way he walks, his dark skin.*

The boy who looked like Justin turned his head and stared at me through the window. There was a beeping sound and the train doors closed.

'Justin . . .' I said.

The train pulled away and the boy who looked like Justin was gone, and the real Justin was standing there with a bottle of water in his hand.

'What's the matter with you?' he said. 'You look like you've seen a ghost.'

I didn't know what I'd seen.

I wasn't sure whether to say anything to Justin or not.

I thought maybe not. He didn't believe in that sort of thing anyway.

47

Chapter Thirteen

The entrance to the mosaic was along the platform. There was an anonymous yellow metal door set into the white tiled wall and Justin knocked on it, and a moment later the door opened, and there was a young man, one of the archaeology students I think, wearing a hard hat and he gave us hard hats to wear.

There were three other people visiting the mosaic that day: two elderly women with long white hair who made me think of druids, and an overweight man with a torch on his forehead. We went down an old spiral staircase: it was black, and cast iron, and clanked as we descended. It grew colder and we came to another metal door, and beyond that was a short passageway, and then the space opened up.

We were in a cavern underground. There was no roof

that I could see, only a blackness above us; there was the sound of water dripping, and the air was cold. A door slammed shut behind us. And there was the mosaic: it was four metres wide by eight metres long, lit by standing lights.

It was a two-thousand-year-old jigsaw puzzle: thousands of little square coloured tiles, dyed and baked and cemented into place, and together they all added up to something more – a story told in pictures.

There was no guide so Justin was my guide.

'Orpheus is a musician,' said Justin. 'He plays the lyre, which is kind of like a small harp. I guess he'd play the guitar if you were telling the story today. I guess he'd be a rock star . . . Anyway, he meets a woman called Eurydice and she's beautiful – she's a supermodel, I suppose – and they fall in love. They're totally in love. Like *forever*. Only she dies.'

'How?'

'Snake bite.'

'Ouch.'

'Yep. Except Orpheus has a plan.'

'A plan?'

Justin nodded. 'She's dead. She's in Hades, remember? The underworld. So Orpheus serenades the gods of the underworld. He plays such beautiful music for them that they grant his request. He's allowed to enter the world of the dead so that he can bring Eurydice back to the world of the living.

'Except there's one condition,' Justin continued. 'And I think it's a very strange condition but it's the one the gods of the underworld insisted upon: Orpheus must not look at Eurydice's face until they're safely back in the world of the living. If he looks at her, if he looks upon her beautiful face before they're out of the underworld, the deal's off. Eurydice stays in Hades and Orpheus returns alone.'

We looked at the images of Orpheus with his lyre and of Cerberus, the three-headed dog who guards the exit from the underworld. They were surrounded by female figures who were meant to represent the seasons, but the largest panel depicted Eurydice in the underworld, all done with tiles dyed in different shades of blue.

It was so blue it looked like she was underwater.

It was so blue it looked like she was drowning.

I shivered and the tiles seemed to shimmer.

'And you know what happens next?' said Justin.

'He looks,' I said.

'You've heard it before,' said Justin.

'No,' I said.

'So how do you know he looks?'

'He *has* to look,' I said.

'What do you mean, he *has* to look?'

'It's a story,' I said.

'So?'

'It wouldn't be a story if he didn't look,' I said. 'Something's got to go wrong if it's going to be a story. And not just wrong: it's got to go horribly wrong.'

'It does go wrong,' said Justin. 'It goes horribly wrong. He looks at her, right at the exit from the underworld, and the gods take her back, and Orpheus returns to the world of the living, alone.'

'And that's why we're still hearing about it, thousands of years later,' I said.

'But . . . it's stupid,' said Justin.

'What do you mean, it's stupid?' I said.

'Because all Orpheus has to do is wait,' said Justin. 'Just wait one more minute for the love of his life and then they're out of the underworld. They can be together. They can live happily ever after. But not Orpheus. *Oh no.* He can't wait and it kills *her*.'

I thought about it for a moment.

The two elderly women who'd reminded me of druids

were leaving, I saw.

'I guess it's meant to remind us that we can't cheat death, even if we're special,' I said. 'So it doesn't matter how beautiful you are, or how good you play the guitar, it's not going to save you. It's not going to save the people you love.'

'Maybe that is what it means,' said Justin, walking on. 'But I still don't like Orpheus. There are so many ways he could have played it. He could have said, take me instead so that she can live. He could have said, take my gift, take my music, make me deaf, just let Eurydice live. But he doesn't do anything like that. Instead, he does the one thing they specifically told him not to do, and it kills her.'

'. . . I guess it depends how beautiful she was,' I said.

Justin shook his head. 'Don't,' he said.

'Don't what?'

'Don't make it romantic. It's not romantic. It's stupid.'

I could see his point.

'Anyway,' said Justin, 'it's a story about a *rock star*. I mean, *come on*.'

'And a supermodel,' I said.

'All these stories could be about ordinary people,' said Justin. 'That's where the heroes are anyway, if you think about it. I mean, look at Covid. All those people dying alone. All those doctors and nurses risking their lives trying to save them. That's bravery. That's what being a hero looks like.'

'It is,' I said. I was thinking about my grandmother.

Drops of water fell from somewhere above us and dripped on to the mosaic.

The overweight man with the torch on his forehead had gone, I noticed.

We were alone with the mosaic, deep underground.

I suddenly felt like I wanted to take Justin's hand.

'Maybe we should go,' I said.

'Maybe we should,' he said.

And right then, something went wrong.

Something went horribly wrong.

Chapter Fourteen

There was a strange sound, like a pile of gravel being tipped out of the back of a lorry, and the wall on the far side of the mosaic just kind of tumbled inwards, taking with it one of the standing lights, which sparked and went out. Then came the water, a wave of it coming through the space where the wall had been: Monday's storm and three days of rain weighing down on the ground; it was louder than you thought water could be, and it changed everything forever.

There was cold water at my feet, and it was rising. It was mud-brown, all around: the mosaic was already buried beneath it. Then the water was up to our thighs. Justin grabbed my arm and was pulling me away, back towards the passageway. He turned his phone light on;

suddenly I was ahead of him and he was pushing me forward. 'Go,' he shouted.

Go.

Another wall fell and a wave of water hit us and knocked me down. I tumbled and rolled and swallowed some brown muck, and I was cold; I was surrounded by cold.

Underwater.

Floating.

Nothing to breathe.

Our phone lights floating in the darkness.

There was a moment of air: somehow the wave had washed us into the passage that led to the bottom of the stairs. I was in an air pocket right up against the roof, and I coughed up water, and I saw Justin's face, and he saw me too, and then brown water rose and covered us both. What had been air and light became water and darkness, and what had been oxygen became nothing.

I couldn't work out which way was up, which way was out.

My lungs were bursting.

Somebody was screaming underwater.

Justin was pushing me ahead of him.

Justin was pushing me towards the door at the bottom of the steps.

I heard muffled sounds around me and let out a breath of air from my lungs, the last breath, the breath I'd tried to keep hold of for as long as possible, but I couldn't keep it in, nobody could, and I took a breath of water and there was a feeling of burning, and then a strange feeling of warmth and peace, and I was somewhere else.

Chapter Fifteen

The sign above my head said ALL SERVICES CANCELLED.

No trains.

No people either.

Not a soul.

I was completely alone on the platform at London Bridge station, and now there were no trains home, and no sign of Justin either.

'Justin?' I said.

I had no idea what had happened, or where he could be.

I reached into my pocket for my phone thinking I should call him, but there was nothing in my pockets.

There was a breath of air from the tunnel: cold, stinking

air, and the wind was rising. A scrap of newspaper was picked up by the breeze; it curled in the air like a strange black and white bird.

A worried bird, I thought, *with important news*.

I turned and went quickly back down the platform and along a passageway. I could hear footsteps echoing somewhere nearby – I just couldn't work out where.

'Justin?' I said. 'Justin!'

No answer.

I turned another corner and stopped.

There were three dogs right in front of me.

Three beautiful, dark and golden German shepherds sitting on the floor in the middle of the passageway, looking right at me – staring at me, really – their ears up, alert.

'That's . . . weird,' I said to myself.

'Hi . . .' I said to the dogs. I gave a little wave.

They didn't move.

I took a step towards them and the dog in the middle . . . stood up.

I stopped and waited.

I took another step and the dog *growled* at me, and I stopped.

Another step, another *growl*.

One more step and the dog barked, and the other dogs stood up, too.

'OK,' I said. I wasn't moving now. 'Just, just, just stay calm . . .'

I started backing away from them.

They didn't move, but their eyes stayed on me all the time.

I turned and walked on, and I didn't hear them coming after me.

*

There was only one way to go it seemed – back to the platform – but when I got there it wasn't there any more.

The station had flooded. The water was clear like rainwater. The flood had found its level, flush with the edge of the platform. The sooty black rail pit was full to the brim with water, and I saw the electric rails spark and burn themselves out.

I was standing by a river. The platform was the riverbank and the water streamed by, flowing east to west. Little tides of water washed back and forth at my feet, soaking my trainers.

The water was warm. I felt a wave of calm inside me.

There was a pattering sound behind me and the dogs

appeared, but I felt no fear. They came to me and sniffed around me, one at my feet, one at my hand, while the other stood on its hind legs and put its paws on my chest so it could sniff my face, my mouth, my breath.

This is the one, their thoughts whispered.

This is she.

Take her.

Then one of the dogs barked, and I turned.

Something was coming out of the tunnel.

It was a boat.

A plain old wooden boat with a boatman.

I remembered what Justin had told me about the ancient Greeks.

About what they believed happened when you died.

The boatman was Charon and the dogs, I realised, were versions of Cerberus, the three-headed dog who guarded the way out of the underworld.

The river was the Styx.

It was the river of death, and I was dead.

Chapter Sixteen

Charon threw out a rope, and the dogs picked it up between their teeth and held the boat in the water, against the current.

Charon stayed where he was, standing in the boat, looking at me, waiting.

He was an old man, his face weathered from years of work on the river, his short white hair spiking up. His skin, amidst his black cloak, was tattooed.

A sailor, I thought.

No. A pirate.

A navigator on full dark seas and never once lost.

Someone chosen from humanity for the final task.

'Take my hand,' he said, and I took his hand. There was no thought in it, no decision, and with my hand in his I stepped into the boat.

'Sit down,' he said, and he pointed to the stern where there were blankets and a pillow. Then he picked up his punt, a long wooden pole for guiding the boat, and the dogs leaped aboard with the ropes between their teeth, and now that there was nothing to tie us to the old world any more, we departed.

The dogs settled around me; one curled up to go to sleep, another watched the water, while the other eyed me with brown friendly eyes.

We came to the mouth of the tunnel at the end of the platform, and the darkness received us. There was a moment when all I could see was the dog's eyes, glowing amber with a strange inner light, and all I could hear was water all around, and then the darkness released us and we were passing under a stone archway overgrown with ivy and gliding silently out into the light.

It was summer.

We were on a river.

*

Swifts came *screeing* from the trees as if they were telling the world we'd arrived. Fish broke the surface of the water around the boat, and then the river quietened. There were willows at the water's edge, and woods of yew and oak beyond, and above it the sky was a vibrant blue with only a few clouds.

There was a sense of peace.

I lay back in the boat and let my hand trail in the water and watched the treetops passing overhead. The sunlight came in dappled pools and every now and then I heard the sound of Charon's punt in the water, steering us along.

I leaned over the side of the boat and looked down into the water. Reeds billowed from a silty bottom a metre and a half below. Shafts of sunlight came and went, and there were sticks and white stones poking up out of the mud.

Except they weren't sticks or stones, I realised.

They were bones.

Down there in the silt was a human ribcage with reeds growing up through it. Next came a jawbone with nearly all its teeth, and nearby was the skull it had belonged to looking up at me with empty eyes.

I looked at Charon at the front of the boat punting onwards.

Where was he taking me?

I looked at the dogs; they were watching the riverbank, ears up, alert.

What were they watching for?

Was there something out there, something we should be afraid of?

I turned and looked back the way we'd come.

There was something in the sky over there, very small and very far away.

A small red dot moving in the air.

A kite.

My kite.

But who was flying it, if not me?

Chapter Seventeen

We came to an old wooden jetty and tied up. The dogs disappeared, running off into the trees on the trail of something or other. Charon stowed his punt in the boat and held out a hand to help me ashore, and I took it.

There was an old black iron stove on the jetty but it wasn't lit. Instead, from somewhere in the folds of his long black cloak Charon brought out an orange-and-brown hot-water flask – the sort of thing my grandmother would have owned. He took the top off and unscrewed the lid, and poured steaming black coffee into the cap.

'Here,' he said, offering it to me.

I didn't move. I didn't know what to say.

'You're in shock,' he said.

Yes, I thought.

I'm in shock.

'This will help,' he said.

I took the cup from him and tasted it. The coffee was dark and rich and powerful and something in me awakened and I drank it all down quickly.

When I'd finished, he said, 'More?'

I nodded and he filled my cup again.

I drank.

Charon said simply, 'Speak now.'

All right. 'Where's Justin?' I said.

'Justin?'

'My friend. He was with me when I . . . when we . . .'

Charon nodded. 'Your friend has gone on ahead,' he said.

'Will I see him again?'

'It depends.'

'On what?'

'On him. He may wait for you. He may not. I don't know.'

I remembered what Justin had told me about the ferryman, about the fare to cross the river.

'I don't have any money,' I said. 'I don't have a coin. I can't pay you.'

'There's no fare for children,' said Charon. He got to his feet.

Children go free. It made a kind of sense.

Charon took the cup from my hands and rinsed it in the river and dried it with his cloak and put it back on top of the flask.

The dogs barked; they were making their way back to the boat.

'There's a path you must take,' said Charon.

'Where?' I said.

'A path through the woods,' he said, pointing.

I nodded. The dogs came running back.

'Go,' he said. 'Go now.'

'Thank you,' I said.

Chapter Eighteen

There was a path through the woods, as Charon had said: foot-worn, bare, hard earth. There were no other paths; it was clear which way I had to go.

I was in a centuries-old forest of oak and beech and yew. There were briars with small pink flowers and there was birdsong in the branches above, and moss sleeping on rocks, and sunlight fell gently here and there.

After a while the path began to climb and went on climbing, and the forest thinned out to reveal the sky, and I walked beneath tall elegant pines. The trail went this way and that through the trees and I glimpsed a patch of colour ahead.

A patch of orange.

Justin's cagoule.

I broke into a run.

'Hey!' I called. 'Justin!'

I ran through the trees and came up the rise, and there was Justin, sitting on a large rock – a boulder really – at the side of the path. He had his arms folded over his knees and he was wearing his glasses.

'Hi,' he said quietly. He had waited for me and I was glad.

'Hi,' I said.

He stepped down from the boulder.

For a moment we just looked at each other.

'We're dead, aren't we?' he said.

I nodded.

'We drowned.'

'Yes.'

'You're sure?'

'I'm sure,' I said. 'No one could have got out of there.'

'No,' he said. 'I don't suppose they could.'

He sat down on the ground in the middle of the path and covered his face with his hands.

'I wasn't sure,' he said. 'Even afterwards . . . I wasn't sure.'

I waited. He took several deep breaths, as if he was on the verge of having a panic attack, and then he was still. He took his hands away from his face and looked at me.

'I'm sorry,' he said.

'I'm sorry too,' I said.

'I mean, I'm sorry about everything,' he said. 'It's my fault you were there.'

For a moment I didn't know what to say.

'It was an accident,' I said. 'You couldn't have known what was going to happen. No one could. You don't have anything to be sorry about.'

'But I am,' he said, and I could see he meant it. 'I am sorry.'

*

We went on along the path through the trees. I walked ahead, and Justin followed, dragging his feet, deep in thought.

After a while he said, 'Where do you think we are?'

'I don't know,' I said. 'The underworld I guess. Something like that.'

'And where do you think we're headed?'

'I don't know,' I said. Then I said, 'What are you asking me for anyway? I had the flu, remember? I missed those lessons. You're the one who's supposed to know about the river and the ferryman and the oblong.'

'Obol,' he said. 'It's called an obol.'

'But we didn't need it, did we?'

'No,' he said. Then he stopped and looked back the way we'd come.

'Something's wrong,' he said.

I stopped, too. 'What do you mean?'

'I mean something's not right,' he said. He was looking all around him, at the trees, at the sky, at the path, thinking hard. 'I can't explain it. I can't put my finger on it. It's just a feeling. Something doesn't make sense and I don't know what it is.'

He looked at me. 'Does this feel right to you?'

'It feels like a forest,' I said. 'It feels like a path.'

He nodded, unconvinced, and we went on.

Chapter Nineteen

Justin was quiet for a while after that. Above the trees, the sky was blue with just a few high clouds, and the sunlight felt warm. The sounds of the forest – birdsong and breeze, and every now and then the sound of water trickling over rocks – were calming.

As was the simple rhythm of our feet.

Time passed, and the path climbed higher and higher.

Then we came to something that didn't make sense.

Something that looked out of place here.

We stopped.

It was a box.

A cardboard box, on the ground, in the middle of the path.

It was strangely familiar; it looked like one of the boxes

from the den back home. It looked like one of the boxes that had come from Grandma's house after she died. But it couldn't be one of those boxes, could it?

'What do you think it is?' I said.

'It's a box,' said Justin.

'I know it's a box,' I said. 'I mean, what's it doing here?'

'I've no idea,' said Justin.

He walked up to it and I followed.

'I guess we have to open it to find out,' he said.

I nodded. 'I think we're meant to open it,' I said. 'I think it's for us.'

We looked at each other. Then we opened the box.

There was something inside it.

Two things actually.

Two Walkmans, a blue one and a yellow one, with two sets of headphones.

Justin picked up the blue one. 'What is it?' he said.

'It's a Walkman,' I said.

Justin looked at me. 'What's a Walkman?' he said.

'It's a personal music player,' I said. 'Like your phone, except from before they had phones.' I picked the yellow one up. 'It's supposed to be light enough to carry around with you. To walk around with it.'

It was exactly like my dad's old Walkman, only his was

blue like the one Justin had in his hands. There were buttons down the edge and a clear plastic window on the front; I could see that there was a tape inside.

I pressed eject and the window snapped open, and I took out the cassette. It was a blank tape, and there was something written on the label in spidery black handwriting.

Justin Fletcher.

I turned the tape over and there was Justin's name again.

'Justin . . .' I said.

'What?'

'This has got your name on it,' I said.

I showed him the tape, and he looked at the Walkman he was holding, and pressed a button, and the tape popped out, and someone had written on that one too.

Justin showed it to me. 'It's got your name on it.'

Eleanor Newton.

Just that. Just my name. In the same spidery black handwriting.

'Weird,' said Justin.

'It is,' I said.

I had a creepy feeling then, and I could not put my finger on what it was, what it meant. It was an idea, a thought – but the thought or the idea seemed to vanish as soon as I tried to grasp it. It was something to do with the cardboard box and the Walkmans, which were very much like things I knew in the real world, in the world of the living. And then there was the river and the boatman and the shadow world, which Justin had told me about. But try as I might I couldn't connect all these things together into a single story, a single idea.

'We have to listen to these tapes,' said Justin, and the idea I'd been trying to catch hold of slipped away.

'I know,' I said.

We swapped tapes. I took the tape with my name written on it, and slotted it into the yellow Walkman, and Justin took the tape with his name on it and put it into the blue Walkman. Then we reached for the headphones – spongy foam earphones on either end of a black plastic hoop – and put them on.

I pressed play and the wheels inside the Walkman started turning.

First there was simply *hiss*.

Then there was a voice.

'Before we begin,' said the voice, 'we need to make sure you are who we think you are. We need to be absolutely sure that we haven't made any mistakes.'

The voice sounded familiar.

Very familiar.

The voice sounded like *me*.

It *was* my voice.

I was talking to myself.

Justin gestured to his headphones and said, 'It's me. It's my voice.'

'Same here,' I said.

'Say your name,' said the voice, between my ears.

I said my name out loud, and a moment later so did Justin.

'Tell me your date of birth,' said the voice.

I said my date of birth.

Then the voice said simply, 'Welcome.'

'Thank you,' I said. I didn't know what else to say.

'What now?' said Justin.

'Follow the path,' said the voice, my voice.

'Where are we going?' I said.

'The path will take you to your destination,' said the voice between my ears. 'The great journey continues.'

Chapter Twenty

After half an hour of walking, and stony silence on the Walkmans – which made me wonder if the voices would ever say anything again – we came to a fork in the road and stopped.

The path split: one fork went left, down the hill, and the other went right, up the hill.

'Take the path to the left,' said the voice between my ears, 'down the hill and into the valley.'

I looked at Justin and pointed to the left.

He shook his head. 'Mine says go right,' he said.

'Mine says go left,' I said. 'Are you sure yours says go right?'

'I'm sure,' he said. 'Are you sure yours says go left?'

'Take the path to the left,' the voice repeated in my ears.

'I'm sure,' I said.

We looked at each other.

I can't, I thought.

I can't go.

'I don't think I can do this,' said Justin.

'Why?' I said to the voice on the tape. 'Why are you sending us in different directions?'

'I have the same question,' said Justin – to the voice on his tape. 'You heard her. Why are you splitting us up?'

There was no answer, only a distant buzzing sound between my ears.

'What if we don't split up?' I said. 'What if we pick a path and we go together?'

'You cannot,' said the voice between my ears.

'It says we can't,' I said and Justin nodded.

'Will we see each other again?' I said.

The voice was silent for a moment – and then it answered, 'It's unclear.'

'It's unclear,' I repeated.

'Same here,' said Justin.

I took my headphones off and Justin did the same.

We looked at each other.

'Let's go the same way,' he said.

'That's just what I was thinking,' I said.

We set off together down the left fork at quite a pace. I could hear Justin's footsteps alongside mine on the path and I was aware of him beside me, at my shoulder, and then there was a strange kind of silence and I became aware of his absence, and when I stopped to look, he was gone.

'Justin?'

No answer.

I walked back up to the fork in the path, and there was Justin, walking back down the path to the right.

'What happened to you?' I said.

'Nothing,' he said.

'But you disappeared,' I said.

'I disappeared?' he said. '*You* disappeared.'

We looked at each other.

'Let's try it again,' I said. 'The right fork.'

We set off together up the hill, and it was the same as before. One minute he was right there, walking a few steps in front of me, and the next . . . I must have blinked or looked away or something, because he was suddenly gone.

'Justin?'

No answer.

'Justin!'

I walked back down to the fork in time to see Justin

walking back up the other path towards me. He looked at me, and then he sighed and said, 'I'm sorry, Eleanor.'

We were both thinking the same thing.

We can't do it.

We can't go the same way.

'I guess this is goodbye,' said Justin.

'I guess so,' I said.

For a moment neither of us said anything.

'I don't know what to say,' said Justin.

'Don't forget me,' I said.

'I won't,' he said. 'I can't, I . . .'

Suddenly he looked right at me. 'I'll look for you,' he said.

'I'll look for you, too,' I said.

Then he held out his hand. For me to shake.

I took his hand and pulled him into a hug, and held him there for what seemed like the longest time.

'Bye then,' he whispered in my ear.

'Bye,' I whispered, and I let him go.

He set off up the path to the right, and I stayed at the fork and watched him go.

I couldn't move. Not right then.

Then, somehow, I turned away, but no sooner had I taken a step towards the path on the left than I heard footsteps quickening, running, behind me.

'Wait,' Justin said. 'Wait, wait, wait . . .'

He was hurrying back down the hill to the fork.

'I'm not thinking clearly,' he said. 'This doesn't feel right.'

'It doesn't,' I said.

'Listen,' he said. 'I got you into this mess and I'm going to get you out of it.'

'How?' I said. 'I mean, what are you going to do?'

'I don't know,' he said. 'But I'm going to do something.'

'Like what?' I said.

'Like . . . Orpheus,' he said

'Orpheus failed,' I said.

'But he didn't have to,' said Justin. 'He nearly did it. And if he nearly did it, I can do it.'

I shook my head. 'You're the smartest person I know,' I said. 'But this is something else. This is . . . the end.'

He shook his head. 'It's not the end. It's . . . I don't know what it is. But I'll find out. And I'll find you, somehow. I'll look for you.'

I sighed.

'Trust me,' he said.

'I do,' I said. 'Kind of. I mean, you're attempting the impossible, but . . . you never know.'

'Exactly,' he said. Then he said, 'Meet me. Meet me here. Tomorrow.' He pointed at the sky. 'When the sun is highest in the sky. I'll be here. I'm going to find us a way out of this.'

He was already on the move, backing away up the path to the right.

'Tomorrow,' he said. 'When the sun is at its highest.'

'Tomorrow.'

'Promise?'

'I promise.'

'See you,' he said, and then he turned and went on, striding away up the path, and I waited there until I was sure he wasn't coming back.

He didn't come back.

I wondered why we'd been sent on separate paths: why the people who ran this place – the gods of the underworld perhaps – had different destinations in mind for us.

I put my headphones on.

'Take the path to the left,' said the voice.

I sighed.

I took the path down the hill and into the valley.

Chapter Twenty-One

I could hear singing coming through the trees: children's voices, far away. Still the path snaked this way and that through the trees, but always down: down the mountain, into the valley. Sometimes there were glimpses of high ridges of pine stretching away into the distance: there seemed to be no end to the country.

I came to a gap in the trees, and stopped.

Down in the valley there was a grand old house made of grey stone. A trail of smoke rose from one of the chimneys; there was a bell tower in the roof. And there were children: dozens of children, running around, and playing sports and games, and walking calmly by themselves, and a choir of sorts was singing a song I was sure I'd heard somewhere before. Beyond the house lay the river, curling away into the distance, and beyond the river the sun hung low and red in the sky; it was the end of the day.

The bell rang and the sound of it sang out through the valley, and I saw it swinging back and forth in its little tower, summoning the children to the house, and in no time at all they had stopped what they were doing and had gone inside, and the grounds lay empty below me.

It was a school; it had to be a school.

I raised the headphones to my ears.

'Is this it?' I said. 'Is this where I'm going?'

'Yes,' said the voice.

*

Twenty minutes later I was down in the valley.

I could see how vast the grounds of the house were. There was a wide grass lawn, which someone had recently mown, and playing fields with grass tennis courts and a basketball hoop hanging from the branch of an old tree and white wood goalposts farther away. Near the school was a garden with ornamental bushes and rockeries and a metal bench under a magnolia tree. Gravelly paths criss-crossed the grounds here and there, but they all led back to the house itself, which was three storeys tall and twelve windows along. There was a semi-circle of stone steps leading up to the front door.

I could smell cooking. The bell had summoned the children in for dinner.

I stopped.

'What is this place?' I said to the voice between my ears.

'This is a way station,' said the voice.

'What's that?' I said.

'A staging post. A resting place for travellers.'

'So it's not actually the end,' I said.

'No,' said the voice. 'In time you'll decide to move on to another place. But that's a long journey across mountain, sea and sky. So take your time. Save your strength. Rest. Reflect.'

The front door opened and a boy of about eight came down the steps kicking a football in front of him. Then came two older girls carrying tennis rackets. I saw that they were all wearing the same kind of clothes. It was a school uniform of sorts: old-fashioned but practical, as if it would do for both games and lessons.

'This is a school, isn't it?' I said.

'A preparatory school, yes,' said the voice.

'Are there lessons?' I said. 'History and maths and so on. Are there exams?'

'No,' said the voice. 'Nothing like that. The time is yours. You're free. This is nothing like any school you've ever been to. This is a breathing space.'

The boy and the girls were walking towards me across the lawn. More children spilled out of the house behind them into the early evening light, and suddenly I didn't want to meet anybody. I didn't want to have to say hello or introduce myself. I didn't want to meet anybody.

I'm not going to fit in here.

'What if I don't want to stay?' I said. 'What if I want to go back?'

'Go back where?' said the voice.

'Across the river,' I said.

'You can't.'

'I know that,' I said. 'I know I *can't*. But what if I *want* to?'

'Look,' said the voice. 'There.'

One of the girls with the tennis rackets had stopped and was staring at me.

'That's Emma,' said the voice. 'Emma was electrocuted.'

And right then – *I saw it.*

The girl called Emma lit up inside. She started to shake and a white light burned through her, illuminating her skeleton like an X-ray. Then the light faded and she was standing in front of me with a thin trickle of black smoke rising from one of her ears.

She turned and walked away.

I let go of the breath I'd been holding in.

'Look again,' said the voice. 'Over there.'

'I don't want to,' I said.

'Look,' said the voice.

It was an order, and I looked.

The boy with the football was staring right at me.

'This is Richard,' said the voice. 'Richard was in a road traffic accident.'

There was the sound of a car horn and a screech of brakes. One moment Richard was there and the next he wasn't. He was flying through the air . . .

He'd been hit by a car I didn't see, a car going way too fast, and he landed six or seven metres away in a lifeless heap.

The football he'd had in his hands rolled down the grass towards me.

'You see,' said the voice. 'You're no different to anybody else. Everyone here is the same: everyone wants to go back. No one does.'

Richard got up slowly. He walked back towards me and I kicked the ball to him, and when he trapped it he looked at me and pointed at the school.

'Go in now,' said the voice between my ears. 'Everything will be all right.'

Chapter Twenty-Two

The front door swung soundlessly open and I stepped into the gloom of the hall.

There was a stained-glass window halfway up the stairs; the last rays of the setting sun made it glow, but that was the only source of light. Below, the walls were covered with dark wood panelling and narrow passages led off in every direction.

There was a small cactus in a pot on a table tucked away in the corner at the bottom of the stairs. By the front door was a stand full of black umbrellas.

There was nobody around.

I took a step and somebody took a step towards me out of the gloom. I stopped, and I saw that the somebody was me. I was standing in front of an old mirror as tall as an archway. It was spotted and stained yellowy-green with age, and looking into it was like looking at myself underwater.

'What do I call this place?' I said.

'This is Eventide House,' said the voice.

Eventide House.

The house you come to at the end of the day.

Right then I realised how tired I was.

'I need to sleep,' I said.

'A room has been prepared for you,' said the voice. 'Take the stairs.'

I went up and the stairs creaked welcomingly. The treads were shiny, worn down by years of use, but I didn't slip. On the first floor the voice said, 'Go on,' and again, on the second floor, and I went on. The stairs narrowed and turned a corner, and then there were three steps down and five steps up, and I was at the top of the house, underneath the roof. The ceiling was lower here and a single passageway with many doors leading off it ran the entire length of the house. *These must have been the servants' quarters*, I thought, *before it was a school, but when was that?*

How old was the house?

And who would they have been the servants for?

I went along the passageway.

'Here,' said the voice.

A door was open; beyond it was a small room.

'This is your room,' said the voice.

I went in. It was bare. There was a blanket folded up on the bed. A thin pillow. A threadbare carpet. But there was a window and a desk with a chair.

I crossed to the window and looked out. It was dusk but I could see the dull silver line of the river curling through the valley. Between the house and river there were vegetable patches: rows of potatoes and carrots, and broad beans tied to sticks. There were also a greenhouse and some small wooden sheds.

'Who built this place?' I said. 'The house, I mean.'

'It's unclear,' said the voice.

'What do you mean it's unclear?' I said. 'Why don't you know?'

'The house was empty when we found it,' said the voice. 'All we know is that people started arriving here. The children started arriving here. The house seemed to have been abandoned. We filled it with life.'

A wave of tiredness crashed over me. I took off my boots and lay down on the bed and rested my head on the pillow. I pulled the blanket over me and lay with the headphones still on my ears and the Walkman on my chest.

I wondered where Justin was. If he'd arrived at a school like this one.

If he was lying on his bed in his room wondering what had happened to me.

'Where's Justin?' I said, but the voice didn't answer me. Instead I heard only softly whispered words: voices praying with a kind of hypnotic gentleness in a language I didn't understand, and behind it all I seemed to hear the sound of the river running by.

Chapter Twenty-Three

Night. Sleep. A sound.

A door opening: the door to my room.

Someone coming in with stealth in the darkness. Someone who didn't want to wake me; someone didn't want me to know they were there. But part of me was awake; I'd been drifting in the shallowest part of sleep, and now there was someone in the room with me.

I panicked but kept my eyes shut. I wanted to see what they were going to do.

It's a woman, I thought – and because I thought that, I wasn't so afraid.

She took a step towards me and the floorboards creaked, but I lay still and let my breath come evenly so she wouldn't know I was awake, and then she came to the bed.

I so wanted to open my eyes. I so wanted to see who it was. But I had to know what she was doing in my room, and why.

She took my hand in hers. Not quite my hand: my wrist.

She put her finger on the vein in my wrist, and I heard a watch ticking close by and I knew what she was doing.

She was taking my pulse the old-fashioned way, counting the beats of my heart while she looked at her watch, and when it was done and she was satisfied, she put my hand back on the top sheet and crept out of the room.

I heard her footsteps stealing away, down the stairs, growing fainter, and then a dark and troubled sleep claimed me for another hour or two.

Chapter Twenty-Four

Birdsong, and a long slow sunrise over the river.

I was already awake, sitting on the windowsill in my room, looking out on the vegetable patch and the land beyond. The sash window was open a crack at the top and I could feel cool air coming in off the river.

I could feel it on my skin; I felt alive.

I needed to pee.

There was an old white tin bowl under the bed and I knew what it was for but I didn't want to use it.

I opened my door. There was no one in the passageway and all the doors were shut. I couldn't hear anyone moving about.

I walked along the passageway to the far end where I found a bathroom. Inside was an old claw-foot iron bathtub stained with rust, and a sink, and a toilet with a huge cistern teetering above it.

I did what I had to do, and then I went downstairs.

*

In the hall there was the smell of freshly baked bread and coffee, and I followed my nose along a short dark passageway and up a flight of steps to a door where a small sign indicated that I was entering the refectory.

It was a large dining hall: fifteen or twenty metres long, with stone arches above and long wooden tables up and down the length of the room. There was no one else there just now, but there was food on the tables: apples and pears, and baskets of fresh bread and pastries, and flasks of coffee.

The sounds of the kitchen came through a serving hatch to one side.

I found a place at the far end of one of the tables and poured myself a cup of the darkest, blackest coffee you've ever seen. Then I grabbed some pastries and a pear and ate my breakfast by myself.

The bell rang somewhere high overhead, and after only a short while I heard movement throughout the house and the children started coming in. They sat down, talking quietly and happily, and ate breakfast.

Strangely, I didn't feel self-conscious at all. No one looked at me; I didn't feel anyone's eyes on me, judging me, or pointing at me and joking about me. I wondered if all that sort of stuff was over now that we were dead.

I hoped it was.

Chapter Twenty-Five

Somebody had been in my room while I was down at breakfast.

There were fresh towels on the bed and a new toothbrush and toothpaste, and a clean set of the school uniform, folded neatly.

I changed into it and looked at myself in the mirror behind the door. It was not entirely a disaster. Everything fitted: the shirt, the blazer, the skirt. It even suited me somehow. It felt comfortable. I felt comfortable in it.

And yet . . . I wanted to keep my old clothes. I thought if I left them lying around here somebody would come and take them away and I'd never get them back again. So I folded them away in the small bottom drawer of the desk, hoping that would send a clear message to whoever had been in here that I wanted to keep them.

Then I sat down on my bed and waited.

There were voices and footsteps on the landing outside, and doors slammed, and gradually the house quietened as the children went off to play whatever games they were going to play today.

When it was completely quiet and I was sure I wasn't going to bump into anybody else, I opened the door and went downstairs.

*

I went exploring; very quickly I realised I was alone in the big house. All the other children were out in the warm sunshine playing games, running around and, from what I could see from one of the upstairs windows, rehearsing a play.

I wandered along dark wooden corridors, trying this door and that, building up a mental map of the layout of the house. Here was the laundry backing on to the kitchens, and the refectory was above them both. Then along the north side of the house I walked through a door into the games room. There was a snooker table and a table tennis table, and benches by the windows where I thought it would be nice to sit and read on a rainy day. There were piles of old board games in their boxes: Cluedo and Monopoly and so on, and on a table in a far corner a game of chess sat waiting, between moves, for the players to return. Also, there was a record player and a pile of old LPs; I decided I would look at them another day.

I went out and wandered through the house, and I came to what could only be the library. There were glass panels above eye level in the door, and through them I could see books on high shelves lining the walls in the room beyond.

I tried the door but it was locked.

I knocked but no one answered or came to open the door.

I wondered who had the key; I would have to ask somebody.

Chapter Twenty-Six

I went out. The sun shone down; children played here and there, and nobody took a blind bit of notice of me. I kept walking, and before long I'd gone beyond the boundaries of the grounds, and the grass grew long on either side of the path. Then I was in the trees again and the path was climbing.

I had an appointment to keep.

I kept walking. The path went this way and that, and the air grew cooler as I climbed. An hour passed. I came to the fork in the path where Justin and I had gone our separate ways.

The sun was at its highest in the sky but there was no sign of Justin. There was a patch of sunlight on a rock to the side of the path and I sat there, watching the other fork, and waited.

And waited.

And waited.

'I'll be here,' Justin had said. 'I'll find a way out of this.'

Except he wasn't here. The sun continued to creep round in the sky. An hour passed, then two, then three.

He wasn't coming. Not today.

What had happened to him? Where had he gone?

I got to my feet. *Perhaps I've missed him*, I thought. *Perhaps I was late. Perhaps he's already been here and gone, but then . . .*

He would have left a message. He would have found some way to let me know he'd been here. And I had to do the same in case he was running late, in case he was on his way here now.

I looked for a stick and when I'd found one that was long enough and sharp, I wrote something on the dry forest floor.

A simple message.

Same time tomorrow.

E.

*

I walked back; when I came down out of the trees into the valley there was a somebody waiting for me, a boy, sitting on the grass by the side of the path.

It was Richard, the boy I'd seen yesterday, the one who'd been hit by the car.

He got to his feet as I approached.

'You're Eleanor, aren't you?' he said. 'The new girl.'

'Yes.'

'You're to come and see Mrs Cauke,' he said.

'Who's Mrs Cauke?' I said.

'The headmistress.'

Chapter Twenty-Seven

We came to a door at the end of a dark wooden passageway and Richard knocked on it.

'Enter,' said a voice from beyond.

I opened the door and went in. A woman looked up from behind her desk.

'That will be all thank you, Richard,' she said. 'Pull the door to, would you?'

The door closed behind me.

I looked at Mrs Cauke across the desk. There was something hawkish about her dark eyes, and her pale face, and her black hair, streaked with grey. There was something clinical about the way she studied me, as if she was trying to see what I was really like under the skin, as if she was trying to see what I was made of.

Then she seemed to let go of a breath she'd been holding.

'I'm sorry you're here,' she said.

Those were the first words she said to me, and somehow I knew she meant it too. No matter how severe she looked, how terrifying, there was something else there: some genuine care or concern.

I nodded.

'I'm sorry it's over,' she went on, 'your life in the other world. But we are where we are, you and I, and we're going to have to make the best of it.'

'And where are we, exactly?' I said.

'We are in Hades,' said Mrs Cauke. 'You know that. This is Eventide House.'

'This is a school?' I asked.

'Of sorts,' she said.

'What do you teach here?'

'We don't teach anything,' she said. 'We're not here to transmit knowledge to you. There is nothing to transmit in any case: we know no more about this world than you do. All we know is that children arrive from the other world and stay a while. Eventide House is a way station for impressionable young minds. It's our duty to make the time you spend here as comfortable and as painless as possible.'

'What was it before?' I said. 'Before it was a school?'

'Your guess is as good as mine,' said Mrs Cauke. 'It was empty when my predecessor stumbled upon it. The bushes and trees in the grounds had been allowed to run riot: it was like something out of a fairy tale. I don't think anybody had lived here for a hundred years or more.'

'But where are they, the people who lived here?' I asked, still curious.

'We can only assume that they moved on,' said Mrs Cauke, glancing at her watch. 'As we all do. As you will, when you're ready, in the fullness of time.'

Her watch.

It was Mrs Cauke who'd come into my room and taken my pulse while I slept.

'How will I know when it's time to move on?' I said.

'You'll know. It's a feeling. I'm afraid that's all I'm able to say about it. It's just something that happens. One day you'll wake up and you'll be ready.'

'What happens then? Where do I go?'

'You'll know where to go. Your feet will lead you. The light in the sky will lead you.'

There seemed to be nothing more she could tell me about it. Into the silence that followed came the sound of the school bell, summoning the children.

'The dinner bell,' said Mrs Cauke, and a moment later came the sound of footsteps clomping along the corridors. It all seemed very orderly to me: too orderly, in fact, and I looked at Mrs Cauke and said, 'Are there rules, here?'

'Rules?'

'Things we can and can't do,' I said. 'This is a school. Schools have rules.'

'Not this one,' said Mrs Cauke. 'This world belongs to us. To you. It belongs to the dead, and it's up to us to decide how to live in it.'

'I suppose there have to be some perks of being dead,' I said.

'Quite,' she replied. 'Although we do have customs here at Eventide House. The school bell rings twice a day. Once for breakfast, at about eight in the morning, and once for supper, at about six in the evening. We believe it's good for us all to come together every now and then. But apart from that, you're free. There are lots of leisure activities, none of which are compulsory. I'm afraid there isn't a television set, but even if there was, we wouldn't be able to pick up any transmissions from the other world. There's a record player, I believe, in the games room, and all sorts of board games for rainy days.

Mostly, you'll find, it's sunny here. It's midsummer, give or take a day or two, pretty much all the time, and if all you want to do is lie on the grass, you're welcome to.'

'I see.'

'One more thing. The chapel is out of bounds at present. Problems with subsidence I believe. We're having some work done. It will be rectified shortly.'

It hadn't occurred to me there would be a chapel here.

'Any questions?' said Mrs Cauke, and I realised there was one.

A burning question.

The only question.

'There's a friend of mine,' I said. 'Justin Fletcher. Do you know where he is?'

'Justin Fletcher,' she said, trying to work out if she had heard the name before. 'Justin Fletcher . . . no. Sorry. There's no one here by that name.'

'He was with me in the forest. We went separate ways.'

'I see,' said Mrs Cauke. I thought I saw her wince.

'But where else could he have gone?' I said. 'I mean, where else is there?'

Mrs Cauke looked at her hands for a moment. 'We can't always be with the people we would like to be with our entire lives,' she said. 'I'm afraid I don't have any information about your friend. I don't know where he could be.'

'But where else is there?' I said.

'There is only Eventide House,' said Mrs Cauke. 'As far as we know.'

I'm going to need a map, I thought.

Mrs Cauke looked at her watch again. 'You'd better hurry and get something to eat,' she said, 'before it's all gone.'

Chapter Twenty-Eight

I joined the end of the queue by the serving hatch in the refectory and picked up a bowl and inched forward along with everyone else. There were older children working in the kitchens, I saw, and one of them gave me some vegetable stew and a chunk of bread, and I went and found somewhere to sit down. I ate, and found myself looking at the boy sitting opposite me, and I saw that he was tired out from a day spent running around, and entirely content. All the children were content it seemed. They were strangely quiet; there was the *chink* of plates and cutlery, but there was hardly any talk.

It felt more like a monastery than a school.

I wondered if that was the point of all these games: to tire us out, to make us forget where we were and why we were here, to help switch off that part of our brains that was thinking, thinking, always thinking.

To induce a monastic, dream-like calm.

I had to admit it was peaceful, this calm.

The soup was done; then little bowls of fresh strawberries appeared at the hatch, and some of the older children brought round flasks of tea and coffee to the tables.

Mrs Cauke appeared and took a cup of coffee, nothing more, and sat down on a plain wooden chair to one side.

I realised I'd forgotten to ask her for the key to the library.

'May I have your attention, please?' said a female voice, and I turned and saw a young woman with dark hair standing at the far end of the refectory. Behind her, on the dais, some children were putting up stage trees: painted props made of cardboard.

'I'm Miss Simmons,' said the woman. 'But you can call me Rachel. I help out with our very own Eventide House Theatricals, and tonight, for one night only, I have great pleasure in welcoming the players . . .'

Behind her a troupe of children of all ages in odd costumes had lined up.

'. . . to perform for you a little play by the name of

A Midsummer Night's Dream . . .'

Around me the other children started thumping on the table with their fists and stamping their feet, and I realised I was too tired to sit through a play.

Another night perhaps.

All eyes were on the play, and I slipped away to bed.

Chapter Twenty-Nine

Something woke me in the middle of the night.

One moment I was in a deep sleep, and the next *whoosh!*
My eyes were open in the dark.

I lay there wondering what it was that had woken me.

Then I realised nothing had woken me: I'd woken myself. I was awake because my body thought it was morning already.

I had *jet lag*.

There must be a time difference between this world and the other. Not much, a few hours perhaps – as if you'd travelled between Europe and America – but because my body still thought it was in the old world, it was enough to wake me up.

There was nothing to be done about it; it would pass

in a couple of days. I got out of bed and opened the curtains and looked out on the dark shape of the land going down to the silvery river below.

I didn't think I'd be able to get back to sleep.

I was hungry again too.

*

The lamps were out in the passageway and on the stairs, and I went down dreading the creak of the treads, but they made no sound, and by the time I was at the bottom my eyes had adjusted to the dark and I could see my ghostly reflection in the great arched mirror in the hall.

I waited. I listened.

Everybody was asleep.

I crept along the passageway to the refectory and tried the door, and it opened, and I found myself standing at the end of the long empty space. Moonlight fell through the windows on the west side, and the painted trees on the dais at the far end looked like eerie, frozen statues.

I went to the serving hatch and saw that it was closed: padlocked in fact.

I left the refectory and tried to remember where the kitchens were, in the dark. I went left along one passageway, then right along another, and then I was lost.

But there was a light.

A faint light, and I realised where I was: I was outside the library.

Light glowed beyond the glass panels set high in the door: a low light, warm, like a lantern. I went to the door and stood on tiptoe, trying to look in, but I wasn't quite tall enough, and when I tried the door, it was still locked.

I knocked quietly and waited. I didn't want to wake up the whole house. Then I knocked again and watched the light through the windows above.

It went out.

Someone had put out the light. Someone didn't want anyone to know they were in the library.

*

I still couldn't sleep. I wandered through the house, adding to my mental map of the building. I found the kitchens eventually (they were locked) and then I worked my way back to the hall.

I sat on the bottom of the stairs for a while, and then I dared myself to touch the little cactus on the table in the corner there and pricked my finger.

It hurt.

A bit. But not much. Not really.

To be honest I was a bit bored.

I've wound up in the boring version of Hades, I thought. *For boring people.*

Just my luck, I thought. *This is going to be fun.*

I got up and went to the front door and tried the handle.

It opened without a sound and I stepped out into the moonlight.

I walked out into the grounds.

Crunch, crunch, crunch went my feet on the gravel, and then I stepped on to the grass and went on more quietly. I didn't want anyone to hear me, or see me, although I was pretty sure I wasn't breaking any rules being up this late or being outside.

Unless there were rules Mrs Cauke hadn't told me about.

I walked between the ornamental bushes and rockeries and stood beneath the magnolia tree. Then I looked back at the house, and there, in one of the windows downstairs, was a light.

The library again.

All the other windows were dark; the rest of the house was asleep. But whoever had put out the light in the library had lit it again. They were awake and up to something, and while I didn't want to bother them, I really did want to get my hands on a map.

A map of the valley and the river and the mountains.

A map that would show me where Justin's path had taken him.

I went back through the garden and crossed the grass that lay like a green moat around the house to the window with the light in it.

It was a little high off the ground but I could reach the windowsill with my fingers. I found a foothold where a drainpipe was attached to the wall by a strut of metal, and I pulled myself up and got my elbows on the narrow ledge and looked in.

There was somebody sitting at a desk just below the window, with a lantern beside them, working on a big pile of papers. All I could see for now was a head of dark hair.

I knocked quietly on the window and a girl looked up, startled – a girl my age – and then she sighed. She picked up a key that had been sitting on the desk in front of her and showed it to me.

The library key.

I nodded, and the girl nodded. She was coming to let me in.

Then she put a finger to her lips. *Shh.*

Chapter Thirty

The key turned in the lock and the door opened, and a pair of green eyes looked out at me. It was the girl. She had dark hair and freckles. She held up the lantern to take a look at me; then she put a finger to her lips again.

I nodded and the girl looked past me, up and down the corridor, and then she hurried me inside and closed the door behind us.

'What do you want?' she said.

'I can't sleep,' I said.

'You must be the new girl,' she said. 'You're probably jet-lagged.'

'I'm Eleanor,' I said.

'How did you die?' she said.

'I drowned,' I said. 'What about you?'

'I caught a cold,' she said. 'A virus.'

She didn't have to say any more. I knew what had happened to her.

'Well,' she said, 'what do you want?'

'I was wondering if I could borrow some books.'

'Something to take your mind off being dead?'

'Something like that,' I said.

'The library is closed,' she said.

'Well . . . you're here.'

'I'm not here.'

I didn't know what to say to that. Then I said, 'If you're not here, then I'm not here either. In which case you won't mind if I take a look round.'

'Maybe I am here,' said the girl. 'But I work here.'

'Are you the librarian?' I said.

'There is no librarian,' she said. 'I'm the caretaker.'

'I only want to borrow some books,' I said.

'This is a reference library. Not a lending library.'

'That's good,' I said. 'Because I don't actually want to borrow any books. What I'm looking for is a map.'

'A map?' said the girl. Her eyes narrowed. 'Interesting,' she said.

There was a *thump-buddump-buddump* sound from somewhere inside the library, and we turned and looked in the direction it had come from.

'What was that?' I said.

'Books,' she said. 'Books falling off the shelves.'

She walked away, holding the lantern high, deeper into the library, and I followed her. 'It happens all the time,' she said. 'It's almost as if the library is haunted.'

'Haunted?' I said.

'Yes,' she said. 'You know. Ghosts. Things that go bump in the night.'

'I thought we were the ghosts,' I said.

'So did I,' she said. 'But sometimes I'm not so sure . . .'

We turned a corner and stopped. A little pile of books lay on the floor beneath a bookcase; above, there was a gap on the shelf from which they had fallen.

'It's almost as if they were pushed,' said the girl, bending down to pick up the books. She looked at the titles on the covers. 'This is one of their favourites.'

'One of whose favourites?' I said.

'The ghosts,' she said, showing me the book in her hand. It was an old, worn, illustrated edition of *Sleeping Beauty*, the fairy tale by the Brothers Grimm.

'Who do you think they are?' I said.

'Who?'

'The ghosts.'

She put the book back on the shelf with the others. 'I think they're the people who lived here before,' she said. 'Before it was a school. Before the children started coming here. It's almost as if they're still here somehow . . .'

She stopped and stared at me.

'Don't you think it's strange?' she said. 'All this. The house and everything.'

'I think it's very strange,' I said.

'Good,' she said. 'So do I.'

'I have questions,' I said. 'At least, I think I have questions. Except I'm not quite sure what they are. How to put it into words, exactly. I suppose what I mean is I want answers, and the answers will tell me what the questions are . . .'

'Exactly,' said the girl, and she looked away from me into the darkness of the library. 'That's exactly it. That's why I'm here. The answers will be here if they're anywhere, in the library. Somebody will have left a trail of breadcrumbs.'

She looked at me. 'There are no maps,' she said. 'But there are photographs. Come on, I'll show you what I've got.'

*

Her name was Ash, she said. She poured two small cups of coffee from a flask; we were sitting at a desk in a deep recess somewhere near the heart of the library.

There were all sorts of books and papers on the shelves near by, and old box files. There was the smell of dust in the air.

'I've been trying to find out something about the history of Eventide House,' she said. 'Who built it, and when and why? And what happened to them? Where did they go? Why did they leave? What was this place before it was a school?'

She reached for a box file and put her hands on top of it.

'All I've been able to find so far,' she said, 'are these.'

She opened the box and took out a pile of old black and white photographs.

'Here,' she said, placing them in front of me. I picked up the first picture: it was an aerial photograph of Eventide House, taken from thirty or forty metres up in the air. You could see the roof of the house, but the grounds were hidden by a forest of trees and bushes that had been allowed to grow up around it; the house would have been almost invisible if you'd approached it on foot.

I wondered how this photograph had been taken.

'A kite,' said Ash. 'Or a balloon. In case you're wondering.'

I looked at her, wondering if she'd just read my mind, and she looked away and slid more pictures across the table towards me. I saw photographs of the land around the house being cleared: trees lay where they had been felled and bushes had been ripped up, and the house appeared beyond them, more or less as it was today.

'These photographs were taken by the people who founded the school,' said Ash. 'This is the house as it was when they discovered it.'

'What was it like before?' I said.

'We don't know. This is all I've been able to find. Here. These are the photographs they took inside the house. This is all we have to go on.'

Ash laid out some more photographs. There were pictures of the arched mirror in the hall and an old blackened range in the kitchen, and the refectory, and the library. Then there were photographs of empty rooms: bare, abandoned rooms. There was a picture of a spinning wheel in the corner of a room, by a window, with a spindle lying on the floor nearby. Then there was a picture of a strange stone room.

'What's that?' I said.

'That's the chapel,' Ash said.

I looked at it: it was round, with what looked like a well in the middle of it, and some old wooden pews arranged in a circle around the well.

'It doesn't look much like a church,' I said.

'It's old,' Ash said. 'Really old. It's more of a temple than a church.'

'It's closed at the moment, isn't it?' I said. 'For repairs.'

'It's been closed for as long as anybody can remember,' said Ash.

There was a sound somewhere above us, then, and we looked up.

Footsteps going along one of the passages upstairs.

Somebody was awake.

'Who's that?' I said.

'Miss Simmons, the drama teacher,' Ash said, looking up, listening to the sound of movement above. 'I don't think she sleeps too well. She's often up in the night. She's on her way down to the refectory to make one of her special teas.'

We were silent until the footsteps had passed.

'You should go,' said Ash. 'Before you bump into her. She'll put the kettle on in a moment – while it's boiling she won't hear you going back upstairs.'

'What about you?' I said. 'Aren't you going back to bed?'

She nodded. 'We should go separately. It's easier to explain if anybody sees us. Besides, I don't think they like people digging around in the library, so I'm going to ask you not to tell anyone you've been here with me.'

'All right,' I said.

'No one,' she said. 'Please.'

I nodded. 'Can I come back tomorrow night?'

It was agreed: if I woke in the middle of the night, I could come back. There was a sign; I was to knock four times and Ash would let me in.

I crept out and along the passageway – I stumbled in the dark once or twice – and then I came to the hall and stole back up the stairs to bed.

Chapter Thirty-One

I slept late; the breakfast bell woke me, and when I went downstairs the refectory was already busy with children getting their breakfast. I looked for Ash but I didn't see her anywhere, so I downed a cup of black coffee and pocketed a pastry and a bread roll for later, and then I slipped out.

Out through the hall, and out of the front door into the grounds.

It was still cool outside. There was dew on the grass, and only the sound of my feet on the gravel path – *crunch, crunch, crunch.*

I was determined not to miss Justin today.

I made my way across the grounds to the treeline and walked on.

*

I knew as soon as I approached the fork in the path that something was different. I could see my own message written on the forest floor with a stick.

Same time tomorrow.

E.

But underneath it someone had written, in a shaky hand, a single word:

Listen.

Justin. It had to be from Justin. He had been here yesterday, after I'd left, or in the night maybe. But what did it mean?

Listen now?

Listen for what?

I looked at the forest around me and listened. There was the sound of the wind in the leaves on the trees and distant birdsong, but nothing else that I could hear.

I sat on the sun-warmed rock and waited, watching the path to the right. There was no sign of Justin. No sign of what I wanted to see most in all the world: just *him*, walking down the hill with a smile on his face and a plan for getting us out of this mess.

I looked again at the word on the ground.

Maybe he means the Walkman, I thought.

Maybe there's something on the tape.

Something I need to hear.

The wind dropped then, and in the silence that followed there *was* a distinct sound, and I held my breath and listened.

Water trickling over rocks.

A little brook or a stream somewhere nearby.

I tried to work out where it was coming from.

I stepped off the path.

The forest floor was all rocks and roots and tough prickly briars, but I did not have to go very far before I found the brook. It was hiding in the shade of some rocks, with dark green moss all around it and light green weeds wavering in the water.

Listen.

This is what you wanted me to hear.

I followed the stream down the mountain.

There was something strange about it, I realised: it was going the wrong way. The other river, the Styx, flowed east to west, sunrise to sunset, from the world of the living to the world of the dead.

This stream came from the north. This stream curled back towards the east, gathering strength with every twist and turn.

It was flowing back towards the world of the living.

There was a path beside it now, a foot-worn path, and it

led into a copse of willow trees, and the willows closed over my head. The ground at my feet turned wet and dark; I took another step and my shoe disappeared into the mud, and I stood on one leg and pulled it up out of the swamp.

I took my shoes and socks off and went barefoot through the cold mud.

Squelch, squelch, squelch.

Then I stopped.

There was something hidden in the undergrowth: I almost didn't see it; I almost walked right past it. It was the same colour as the trees and someone had camouflaged it with fallen branches, but it was there all the same.

It was a boat.

I ran to it, sploshing through the mud, and cleared away the branches and stared at it. It was an old wooden rowing boat with two oars and a little bench seat.

I swung myself over the side into the boat and stood up in it, and wondered who had put it here and why.

I looked at the distance from the boat to the river. It would be hard work to drag it out into open water but by no means impossible. An adult could do it, or two children working together. I couldn't do it by myself; I'd need help, unless . . .

Unless it rained.

If it rained, the mud would become the shallows and the shallows open water, and the river would rise to meet the boat.

You could walk the boat out into the river and climb aboard.

Yes.

Someone was waiting for rain. Someone was planning to escape from this world.

Justin, I thought.

This was Justin's plan to get us out of this mess.

Suddenly I was very afraid. My heart was beating like a drum in my chest. I wasn't sure I wanted to go back across the river. I wasn't sure I wanted to be a ghost over there. I wasn't even sure Justin knew what he was doing this time.

*

I walked back to the fork in the path. There was no sign of Justin – just the word he'd written on the ground.

Listen.

I picked up the stick, and underneath his message I wrote:

We need to talk.

E.

Chapter Thirty-Two

My Walkman was gone, I discovered when I got back to the house. I went through the drawers in my room and looked under the bed, but I couldn't find it.

Somebody had been in my room yesterday morning with fresh towels and my school uniform: they must have taken it. But why? And where was it now?

Suddenly I had a lot of questions I wanted to ask the voice on the tape.

*

I knocked on Mrs Cauke's door.

'Enter.'

I went in. She looked up from some papers on her desk.

'It's Eleanor, isn't it?'

'Yes,' I said.

'What can I do for you?'

'I was wondering about my Walkman,' I said. 'It's disappeared from my room. I'm wondering where it is . . . what happened to it?'

Mrs Cauke nodded. 'I'd prefer it if you'd let me look after it.'

'Do you mind if I ask why?' I said. 'I mean, it's mine, isn't it?'

Mrs Cauke hesitated, and said, 'It is yours. But we don't make these machines, you see. Or the tapes. We don't know where they come from or how they get here. And we don't really know how they work. We think it's kind of like the mind talking to itself. Telling you what you need to know to get you here safely. Once you're here, we try to discourage the use of the tapes.'

'Why?'

'It doesn't help,' she said. 'In any way. It can't help.'

'Why not?'

'Because there's nothing on the tapes,' said Mrs Cauke.

'What?' I said. I couldn't believe what I'd heard. 'What do you mean there's nothing on the tapes?'

'I mean exactly that,' she said. 'The tapes are silent. The tapes are blank.'

'I don't believe you,' I said. 'There was a voice. My voice. I heard it.'

Mrs Cauke opened a drawer in her desk and began rummaging around inside it. 'You heard what you needed to hear,' she said. She took out a Walkman and some headphones and a cassette, which she placed on the desk in front of me.

The tape had my name written on it.

'Listen to it,' she said.

I put my tape into the Walkman and put the headphones on and pressed play.

'I'm here,' I said, to the voice on the tape.

Nothing.

'It's me,' I said. 'It's Eleanor.'

Nothing.

'Are you there?' I said. 'It's me, Ellie.'

Nothing.

Just a faint, faraway *hiss*.

'Fast forward it if you like,' said Mrs Cauke and I did, and there was nothing, and I fast forwarded it some more and there was still nothing. Then I turned the tape over and listened, and fast forwarded it again . . .

'You see,' said Mrs Cauke. 'The rest is silence.'

I took the headphones off. I could feel my eyes

smarting with tears.

'I'm sorry, Eleanor,' said Mrs Cauke. 'There never was a voice on the tape. You were talking to yourself the whole time.'

I felt tears rolling down my cheeks. I don't know why I was so upset. It wasn't that I felt cheated. It was more that I was bereft. I felt lost. I felt alone. I just wanted to be home, in the world of the living.

The tape continued to turn inside the machine, and then I pressed stop and pushed the Walkman across the desk to Mrs Cauke.

'Keep it,' I said.

Mrs Cauke nodded.

The bell rang for dinner in the refectory and I went out.

Chapter Thirty-Three

Something woke me in the middle of the night.

Tick tick tick tick

I recognised the sound.

It was my grandmother's watch.

Tick tick tick tick

It was right there in the room with me.

It was right there on my wrist.

Tick tick tick tickTICK TICK TICK TICK.

I opened my eyes, and the room was silent.

I reached for my wrist.

No watch.

But I was awake.

*

The house was dark and everybody else was asleep. I went downstairs in my socks this time, not wanting to make a sound, and knocked four times on the library door and waited.

A light appeared, and the key turned in the lock and the door opened a crack.

'It's me,' I whispered.

Ash grinned and pulled me inside and locked the door after us. For the first time I noticed she wasn't wearing the school uniform: she was wearing her own clothes – the clothes she'd brought with her from the world of the living.

'Follow me,' she said, and she set off through the library with the lantern, and I followed. She stopped in front of a bookcase I thought I recognised from last night: it was the one from which the books had tumbled to the floor.

'What I'm going to show you is top secret,' she said.

I nodded.

'You need to swear not to tell,' she said. 'You need to swear your best promise. You need to swear on your life and on your death.'

'I do.'

'You have to say it,' she said.

'I swear,' I said, 'on my life and my death I will not tell.'

Ash nodded. Then she put her hands on the bookcase and pushed, and the bookcase swung silently aside, just like a door, and beyond it was a small room. There was a makeshift bed on the floor and a table with a pile of books.

'A secret room,' I said.

'A secret room in a library,' said Ash, and we stepped inside.

'It's like something out of a story,' I said. An idea was fluttering around my head again: I couldn't pin it down.

'It's exactly like something out of a story,' said Ash, pulling the secret door shut behind us. 'It's almost as if this isn't a real house at all. It's as if the house shapes itself around us, around the things we love, and the things we believe about life and death and the afterlife . . . Maybe even the books we've read.'

I looked at the room. 'I don't know,' I said. 'It seems pretty real to me.'

There was a small square window quite high up, which provided some light during the day. There was a mirror on the wall, and a bowl for washing and some towels and a tube of toothpaste and a toothbrush in a cup.

'You live here,' I said.

'Yes.'

'I did wonder,' I said.

'I don't think they know about me,' she said. 'Mrs Cauke and Miss Simmons. I'd rather you didn't tell them.'

'I won't,' I said. I noticed some cups and plates on the floor, and an apple core.

'How do you eat?' I said. 'I haven't seen you at dinner.'

'I steal,' she said. 'From the kitchens. In the middle of the night. Every now and then I take the dishes back and wash and dry them and put them away in the cupboards.' She looked down at the plates. 'I'm due another washing up session soon.'

'The kitchens are locked though,' I said.

'They are,' said Ash. 'I have a key.'

She reached into her pocket and took out the library key.

'It's the library key,' she said. 'That's all. But for some reason it works in all the locks in Eventide House. It's some sort of master key.'

'Books open all doors,' I said.

'Something like that,' said Ash.

There was a *thump-buddump-buddump* sound, and we looked at each other.

'The ghosts are back,' Ash said. She turned and pushed the secret door open and stepped out into the darkness.

A moment later she was back with a book in her hands. She closed the door and handed the book to me.

Sleeping Beauty.

'Someone wants us to read this, it seems,' she said.

It was the same book that had fallen off the shelf the other night, and now that I held it in my hands I could see that it was a hardback, quite old and lavishly decorated. There was a picture on the cover of the princess lying down, eyes closed, surrounded by flowers and vines and trees. It reminded me of the picture of Ophelia my grandmother had taken me to see at Tate Britain before she died, although Ophelia had drowned of course, while the princess in *Sleeping Beauty* was merely sleeping.

There was no author listed on the cover or inside.

'You know the story,' said Ash. 'Everybody does. There's a princess and she pricks her finger on a spindle, and she falls into a sleep that lasts for a hundred years.'

I knew the story. 'Then a prince comes to the castle and he kisses her,' I said.

'He kisses her,' said Ash, 'and she wakes up.'

'And they get married and live happily ever after,' I said.

'That's the version of the story that's usually told, yes,' said Ash.

'Is there another version?' I said.

'There's my version,' said Ash, pouring two small cups of coffee from a flask and handing me one. 'In my version, the princess wakes up and she's furious.

'*Did you just kiss me?* she says.

'*Yes*, he says.

'*On the lips? Without my permission?* she says.

'*Yes*, he says, and he's worried now. He realises what he's done.

'*I'm sorry*, he says.

'*How dare you*, she says. *You're banished. Be gone.*'

'And she meets somebody else,' I said, picking up the thread of the story. 'Somebody she chooses, and *they* live happily ever after.'

'Exactly,' said Ash. 'Because the prince kisses her *when she's asleep*. He doesn't know her. She's never met him before. It's like kissing a stranger in the street.'

'It's worse than that,' I said. 'You can kind of run away from them in the street. This is more like kissing somebody who's in a coma. Somebody who doesn't even know what's happening to them.'

'Exactly,' said Ash. 'Although, I just want to say, if I'm ever in a coma and you happen to be passing, I give you permission to kiss me . . . on the lips . . . just in case it's the

140

one thing that's going to wake me up.'

'All right,' I said. 'I'll kiss you.'

'I'd do the same for you,' Ash said. 'If you want me to of course.'

'I do,' I said, and we looked at each other and smiled and drank our coffees.

*

I took *Sleeping Beauty* back to bed with me and read for an hour or so.

As I was drifting off to sleep I thought, how would I retell this story, today?

Perhaps he isn't a prince, I thought.

Perhaps he isn't a prince and he doesn't kiss her.

Perhaps he's a doctor and he cures her, and that's what it means, this story.

Perhaps the reality behind the fairy tale is an ordinary story of a hospital.

Then I slept.

Chapter Thirty-Four

I woke early again, and went downstairs for breakfast. There seemed to be nobody else around, and I took some coffee and bread and was about to sit down at one of the empty tables when I noticed Mrs Cauke at the far end of the hall.

She was looking right at me, stirring her coffee with a spoon.

She was staring at me.

I walked the length of the hall and sat down in front of her.

'Good morning, Mrs Cauke,' I said.

'Good morning, Eleanor. How are you feeling?'

'Fine, thank you.' I dunked my bread in my coffee.

'Are you sleeping?'

'What's that?' My mouth was full of bread.

'I said, are you sleeping?'

'Yes, I am, thank you. The bed is very comfortable.'

'I only ask,' said Mrs Cauke, 'because we have received some disturbing reports in the night. Some of the children have heard footsteps. Some of the staff have heard voices. It appears someone has been roaming Eventide House in the hours of darkness.'

I stared at Mrs Cauke, and she stared back at me.

'Is that against the rules?' I said.

'No,' said Mrs Cauke. 'But it is discouraged. The soul needs rest. The soul needs a home, which we provide, and now we find that there is a chill in the air. There is something odd going on: food has been going missing from the kitchens. Cups and plates too. I intend to get to the bottom of it.'

I stared at the cup of coffee on the table in front of me.

Ash, I thought.

She knows about Ash.

'Eleanor.'

I looked at her.

'You'd tell me, wouldn't you, if you knew anything about these goings-on?'

The breakfast bell rang, releasing me from her stare.

'I sleep like a rock,' I said. 'I haven't heard anything in the night . . .'

Children began coming in for their breakfast. Mrs Cauke finished her coffee.

'I worry, Eleanor,' said Mrs Cauke, but her eyes were on the other children, as if she was looking for the culprit among them. 'We worry. If there is anything you would like to tell me, what you have to say will be treated in the utmost confidence. We only want you to be happy. We only want you to be well.'

*

I took my time over breakfast and went back for seconds, all to show Mrs Cauke how happy I was, how calm – and as soon as she'd gone I left too, and went to the library to tell Ash what had happened.

I knocked four times but there was no answer. Ash was probably asleep in the secret room with the door closed; my warning would have to wait until tonight.

Chapter Thirty-Five

The sun was high in the sky when I came to the fork in the path and there was no sign of Justin, but there was a message, and the message broke my heart.

Listen, he'd written.

Underneath that I'd written, *We need to talk.*

Underneath that was Justin's reply:

Not coming.

Sorry.

J.

I stared at the message on the ground. I read it over and over again . . . And then I picked up the stick and wrote in the dirt:

Why not?

E.

Because I didn't understand.

Why couldn't he come? Where was he?

He'd been here sometime – when?– and held the same stick as me and written his messages in the dust – and yet he couldn't come and see me?

I looked at the path to the right. I remembered him backing away from me, and I remembered what we'd said to each other.

Tomorrow, when the sun is at its highest.

Tomorrow.

Promise?

Promise.

Now I wondered if I was ever going to see him again.

I sat down on the rock in the sunlight and thought about it, trying to come up with another message to write on the ground, a better message: trying to find the right words, in the right order – the words that would bring Justin here to meet me.

Just so I could see him again.

My mind was blank.

Then it dawned on me.

There was *nothing* I could say – or write – that would bring him back.

But I could go to him.

I picked up the stick and wrote in the dust:

If you're not coming, I'll come and find you.

E.

Then I went back to Eventide House.

Chapter Thirty-Six

The Theatricals were back after dinner in the refectory with another Shakespeare play.

It was *The Tempest* this time: I hadn't known it starts with a shipwreck, and I have to say the children made the storm seem very real, with some noisy sound effects and the sail of the ship rippling in the wind and buckets of water sploshing around on the stage. I was tired but I wanted to stay to watch the play, and I would have done if I hadn't been sitting right at the back – and if I hadn't seen Mrs Cauke and Miss Simmons look at each other across the room and nod.

Some signal must have passed between them, because first Mrs Cauke got up and went out, and Miss Simmons followed a moment later, stepping over me and closing the refectory door behind her.

Hello, I thought. *They're up to something.*

They've gone after whoever it is who's up and about in the night.

I'd better keep an eye on them.

I waited (counting to a hundred in my head) and then I crept out and closed the door quietly, and I stood in the cool of the passageway and listened.

*

There were distant voices and I followed them through the twilight of Eventide House, into the kitchens and along another passageway. I found Mrs Cauke and Miss Simmons in a small room that led off the scullery; they hadn't seen me – I was hidden behind the half-closed door – but they were standing in front of a short row of hooks, and on each of the hooks was a bunch of keys.

Mrs Cauke was counting them. When she'd finished she sighed. 'You see,' she said. 'It's as I expected. There's one missing.'

'You think it's one of the children?' said Miss Simmons.

'I'm sure of it,' said Mrs Cauke. 'No, we must find out who is responsible. We can't have them roaming about the house at all hours of the day and night. We need calm for our researches. The children must remain calm.'

'Do you think perhaps we need to scare them?' said Miss Simmons.

'You may be right,' said Mrs Cauke.

'At least, a little bit.'

'Perhaps we might scare them with the truth?' said Mrs Cauke.

'That can be arranged.'

'At least, some of it,' said Mrs Cauke.

'Very well,' said Miss Simmons. 'I will prepare something for tomorrow night. After supper. Something scary.'

'Something true,' said Mrs Cauke.

Chapter Thirty-Seven

I crept away and up to my room where I fell asleep with the setting sun, and when I woke again it was fully dark and the house was quiet and only I was awake. It was so quiet I could hear the sound of the river running by in the night.

I slunk downstairs in my socks, stopping to watch and listen at every corner, in every doorway. Mrs Cauke knew about Ash – at least she knew that someone was up and about in the night, and it was only a matter of time before she caught me wandering around, and then what would I say for myself?

Nothing, I decided.

I'd pretend I was sleepwalking; there would be nothing to explain.

There was no one on watch tonight it seemed – at least no one saw me – and I came to the library door and knocked four times.

Ash came to the door with her lantern and opened it, and this time it was my turn to put my finger to my lips.

'They know,' I whispered.

*

'It doesn't make any sense,' said Ash when we were in her secret room. 'They keep saying *there are no rules*. There must be a reason they don't want us running around in the middle of the night. What do they think will happen to us? What are they afraid of?'

'That's not it,' I said. 'That can't be it. They weren't worried about us at all. They were worried about something else: their researches, Mrs Cauke said. And she said something about the truth, about only telling us part of the truth, and trying to scare us.'

'. . . It sounds as if they're afraid of us,' said Ash.

'It does,' I said. 'I think they're afraid of what we'll find out if we're up in the middle of the night. I think they're afraid of what we might see.'

'Except,' said Ash, 'there's nothing to see. Trust me.'

'You've been here longer than me,' I said. 'Where haven't you been?'

'Nowhere,' said Ash. 'I've been everywhere.'

'Everywhere?'

'Everywhere,' she said. 'Except the chapel.'

'Which is closed for repairs,' I said.

We looked at each other: we'd both had the same thought.

'Except the chapel,' I said.

'Which almost certainly *isn't* closed for repairs,' Ash said.

Chapter Thirty-Eight

We went along a cold stone passageway and at the end of it was a solid, anonymous oak door. Ash put the library key into the lock and turned, and there was a sound of an iron bolt turning over. She put her hands on the door and pushed and the door opened, and a cold breath of air blew out the candle in the lantern I was holding.

Books open all doors, I thought.

Books unlock all secrets in the end.

I stepped into the cool dark space. There were no windows, only a faint blur of light above us, as if from some primitive chimney. There were shapes to the left and the right – the pews – and something ahead, in the middle of the great round room, directly below the light source in the roof.

The well.

Ash struck a match and lit the lantern again.

I looked up. There didn't seem to be any construction work going on. Nor did there seem to be any structural damage to the chapel itself.

'Mrs Cauke lied to me,' I said.

'To everybody, it seems,' said Ash.

'But why?' I said. 'Why don't they want anybody coming in here?'

Ash didn't answer.

There was the sound, distantly, of something falling into water.

'Did you hear that?' I said.

'Yes,' said Ash. 'The well,' and she went to it, and I followed.

Ash held the lantern out over the well and we peered down into it. We couldn't see anything down there: it was too deep; all was blackness. But we could hear it: we could hear water running quietly below.

Black water.

A river.

Ash held the lantern farther out over the well, and then we saw it, just below the rim, on the inside: a metal ladder stretching down into the darkness, its iron rungs bolted on to the brickwork.

We looked at each other.

Ash smiled.

'No way,' I said, shaking my head. 'No. You can't be serious.'

Ash set the lantern down on the edge and swung her legs over the side of the well and felt around with her feet until she'd found the rungs of the ladder.

'We have to do this,' she said. Then she slipped down out of view. I heard her trainers squeaking on the rungs as she descended.

I leaned out over the well and looked down.

'I'm coming too,' I said.

'Bring the lantern,' she said. 'There's no light down here.'

I climbed over the edge and let my feet find the ladder. Then I descended, dangling the lantern from one little finger as I went hand over hand down the rungs.

Chapter Thirty-Nine

'This is madness,' I said. I could hear the water running darkly below us and I could see Ash a few metres farther down. She was still going down.

'Wait,' she said. 'There's something here . . . I see something.'

'What?' I said.

'A jetty,' she said.

I went down after her and stopped just above her. The well opened up into some sort of cavern at the bottom, and there was a jetty: a narrow, wooden pier, extending only a few metres into the darkness. It leaned and looked as if it might collapse under its own weight at any moment.

There was something on the jetty.

A Walkman attached to a small microphone.

A tiny yellow light on the side indicated that it was recording.

Ash stepped on to the jetty and it creaked and swayed above the water, and then I came down. She put her finger to her lips.

She picked up the Walkman and turned it off.

'It was recording,' she said. 'It isn't now.'

I climbed on to the jetty with her and set the lantern down.

'What do you think it was it recording?' I said.

'I don't know.'

I remembered what Justin had written on the path in the forest. 'Listen.'

Listen.

Then we heard it.

Chapter Forty

It was a gentle whispering at first, like the sound of a river running quietly.

Then gradually it became clear what we were hearing.

We were hearing voices.

Voices from the other world.

They came like whispered prayers.

They were voices of care, and love, and hope, and kindness.

They were voices of love, and loss, and deep, deep mourning.

Every word I heard sounded like HOME to me.

Every word I heard said HOME.

Then the voices stopped. There was the sound of rain all around us, and I held my hand out to see if it was actually raining. Then there was the sound of a train rattling through the London underground, and an ambulance siren, and the sound of a baby crying.

There was music – bars of music I almost recognised – coming and going in the rain, and for a single vivid moment I was back in the world of the living, lying on the floor in the den at home, listening to one of my dad's old LPs while the sunlight moved around the room. Then the record came to an end and the player *clicked* to a stop, and in the silence that followed I heard the ticking of a watch.

Tick, tick, tick, tick . . .

Another sound too. Ash was clicking her fingers in front of my face.

'Wake up,' she said. 'Wake up!'

'I'm here,' I said.

'Where did you go?' she said.

'Home,' I said, and she nodded.

Every word I'd heard said HOME to me.

Every piece of music said HOME.

Even the rain said HOME.

*

It's one thing being dead. It's quite another being reminded of all the things you've lost.

There was nothing Ash could say to me that would make me feel better.

Nothing I could say to her that would make her feel better, either.

We climbed back up the ladder and locked the chapel and went our separate ways into the night. As I was climbing into bed I remember the sound I'd heard in the bottom of the well, the sound of a baby crying, and I thought about Jack, if that was his name, the brother I was never going to meet – at least not for a very long time, not until he crossed the river at the very end of his life.

Would we recognise each other when we met?

Chapter Forty-One

Something happened on my way down to breakfast the next morning.

To be precise, something happened again.

I was at the bottom of the stairs. There was no one else around. But as I passed the great arched mirror, I heard the front door open behind me and I turned, and my grandma walked in.

Grandma, again.

She was in her long grey coat with her umbrella – which she now dropped in the stand by the door. Then she closed the door behind her, and turned and saw me.

Her mouth fell open. 'I've done it again, haven't I?' she said.

'Done what again?' I said.

'I'm early.'

'But . . .'

'I wasn't here, Eleanor,' she said. 'Understand? I was never here.'

She picked up her umbrella. She was already on her way back out the door.

'But Nanna,' I said.

She looked at me. 'I love you,' she said, and then she was gone, closing the door behind her, and I stood there in the hall with my heart thumping away in my chest.

I'd forgotten to tell her I loved her again. *Again, Eleanor.*

I ran to the door and flung it open, but when I did there was only the sunlight on the empty grounds of the house.

No sign of Grandma. No sign that she'd ever been there.

I heard footsteps behind me, the sound of someone on the stairs, and I turned to see that Mrs Cauke had stopped halfway down the stairs, by the stained-glass window.

'Eleanor,' she said. She stared at me, and I wondered if she knew I'd been in the chapel last night.

'Good morning, Mrs Cauke,' I said.

'Has something happened?' she said.

'When?' I said.

'Here,' said Mrs Cauke. 'Now.'

'No,' I said. I pulled the door to, a little guiltily.

Mrs Cauke stared at me. 'Something happened, didn't it?' she said. 'Just now. Something – unusual. What was it?'

'Nothing, I just . . .'

'Tell me,' she said. Somehow she knew that something strange had occurred. I wasn't sure how she knew, but she knew it all right; she sensed it.

'Something happened,' I said quietly.

Mrs Cauke nodded.

'I'll tell you about it,' I said, 'if you'll tell me what's really going on here.'

Mrs Cauke blinked. I'd surprised her; shocked her even. Then she seemed to make a mental calculation and came to a decision.

'Can I trust you, Eleanor?'

'About as much as I can trust you,' I said.

'I'm not sure I like those odds,' said Mrs Cauke. 'But why don't you and I step into my office for a moment?'

Chapter Forty-Two

'I told you we don't teach anything here, and that's true,'
Mrs Cauke said when she'd poured us both a cup of coffee.
'We're not here to transmit knowledge to you. It would be
more accurate to say that you are here to transmit knowledge
to us.'

We were in her office. The bell rang for breakfast;
we ignored it.

'This is more of a research institute than a school,' Mrs
Cauke went on. 'We know no more about this world than
you do. We are all groping in the dark.'

'What are you researching here?' I said.

'Contact,' she said. 'Contact with the other world.'

I thought about the sounds I'd heard in the chapel.

The voices at the bottom of the well.

Voices from the other world.

A kind of listening post.

'We investigate the edge between this world and the world of the living,' Mrs Cauke went on. 'We look for places where the walls are thin. Places where the worlds meet. We believe Eventide House to be one of those places.'

'How?' I said. 'What do you do?'

'We listen,' she said. 'We listen for human voices from the other world. We listen for any sound from the other world that may reach us here. Voices, prayers, radio transmissions. We make recordings. We try to capture these sounds.'

'You use the Walkmans,' I said.

'Yes,' she said. 'But only as recording devices. There really is nothing on the tapes the children bring with them here. But we believe the worlds meet here *because* of the children. It's as if the children have an affinity. Part of the other world seems to cling to them. It's as if they haven't completely crossed over.'

'And what have you found in your research?'

Mrs Cauke looked at her hands. 'The evidence is inconclusive,' she said.

'Inconclusive?'

She nodded. 'We hear things,' she said. 'We record. We listen back – and the sounds we've recorded have vanished. The sounds we thought we heard: the voices, the prayers. We have only our memories of the sounds we thought we'd captured. We have only the evidence of our senses.'

A silence fell between us.

'Tell me what happened to you this morning,' said Mrs Cauke.

I told her about Grandma, about seeing her the day after she'd died, and again, just now, in the hall.

'It's contact,' said Mrs Cauke. 'No doubt about it.'

'But not from the world of the living,' I said.

'No,' said Mrs Cauke. 'From elsewhere in the land of the dead. That's what so puzzling. It's almost as if the two of you have an appointment to keep. But where and when, that's the question . . .'

'And *why*,' I said.

'The why is obvious,' said Mrs Cauke. 'She has a message for you.'

'Does she?'

'Yes. There's something she wants to tell you. But whatever it is, it can only be told at the right time, in the right place.'

'I see,' I said, thinking that perhaps it was me who wanted to say something to Grandma, rather than the other way around. 'And how will I know when it's the right time?'

'You won't,' said Mrs Cauke. 'She will.'

'So what should I do?' I said.

'Nothing,' said Mrs Cauke. 'You don't have to do anything. She will return. She has found you twice. She will find you again.'

Chapter Forty-Three

I went back to the fork in the path.

If you're not coming, I'd written in my last message, *I'll come and find you.*

But what I'd written was gone; all the old messages were gone. Someone had brushed them away and kicked up the dust, and in their place were new messages – or rather a single message repeated over and over again, etched on the path.

Don't follow me.

DON'T FOLLOW ME.

Don't follow me.

Don't follow me.

DON'T FOLLOW ME.

Don't follow me.

DO NOT FOLLOW ME.

Don't follow me.

Don't follow don't follow don't follow don't . . .

I stared at the words on the ground. I could hardly think.

He isn't coming.

Not today. Not ever.

What had happened to him? Where had he gone?

Was I ever going to see him again?

I looked at the path to the right.

'Justin!' I shouted. 'Is that it?'

No answer.

'Is that all you're going to say?' I shouted. 'Is that all you're going to do?'

Nothing.

'You had a plan!' I shouted into the trees. 'You told me you had a plan!'

The echo of my voice fell away in the silence of the forest.

I didn't write anything on the ground: I was too angry with him, too sad and hurt and wounded. I picked up the stick and threw it as far as I could into the undergrowth; I didn't see where it landed. I didn't care. I would never write to him again.

I turned and walked back to Eventide House.

Chapter Forty-Four

After dinner in the refectory there was an announcement about a lantern lecture.

We finished the last mouthfuls of our dessert without a word. Then we remained in our seats and tea and coffee was brought round in small tin cups.

One of the older children climbed a stepladder at the far end of the room while another held it steady at the bottom. The boy at the top hung a large white sheet from the wall, like a cinema screen. Someone else wheeled in a slide projector on a kitchen trolley and placed it between the tables, pointing towards the screen.

It was an old-fashioned electric slide projector, like the ones that sat gathering dust in the stationery cupboard at school.

'Lights,' said Mrs Cauke, and the lights went out.

I remembered the conversation I'd overheard the previous night.

Something scary, Miss Simmons had said.

Something true, Mrs Cauke had replied.

'If you please, Miss Simmons.'

'Thank you, Mrs Cauke.'

Miss Simmons brushed past me in the near darkness and went to the slide projector and turned it on. A beam of blueish light lit up the screen, and dust played in the air above our heads. Then came the *shuffle-click-shuffle-click* sound those machines used to make, and there was the first image.

It was an old black and white photograph of Eventide House in the sunshine, with children playing in its grounds.

'This photograph was taken a hundred years ago,' said Miss Simmons. 'Not long after the school was founded.'

There was a *shuffle-click* and another black and white image appeared on screen. It looked exactly the same as the first one: Eventide House with children playing.

'This photograph was taken last Wednesday,' said Miss Simmons with a smile in her voice. Laughter rippled gently around the room, and she continued, 'You may be wondering why I'm showing you these pictures since all of you already know what Eventide House looks like. The point I'm making is that Eventide House never changes. It is the same today as it was a hundred years ago. It will always be here and there will always be a home for you in Eventide House, should you decide to stay. You are safe here. You are protected here.'

Shuffle-click. Another image. An aerial black and white photograph taken from high up in the air. Below us lay Eventide House and the valley surrounded by wilderness. There was the river. There were the mountains.

'And yet the world we live in is not without danger,' said Miss Simmons. 'Beyond the edges of this photograph there are places and entities we know nothing about. And while we have been lucky here at Eventide House, there have been . . . regrettable incidents. Not everyone who has come to Eventide House has been accounted for.'

Shuffle-click. It was a picture of four girls, all about twelve or thirteen years old, all wearing the school uniform, walking across the lawn below the playing fields.

'These are the lost girls,' said Miss Simmons. 'They vanished before most of you came to Eventide House. We don't know what happened to them; we don't know where they are. We don't know if they even exist any more, in the sense that you or I understand the word "existence". But we do know that they were just like you. They were born and lived in the other world, and they died and came here.

'One of the girls, Jane Torrance, was interested in photography. I let her borrow my camera. She commandeered the old darkroom in the basement. The girls began to spend more and more of their time down there.

'One morning they left the school grounds. We do not know why. We do not know where they intended to go, but they did not return. We could find no trace of them anywhere in the valley or down by the river. Three days later a search party found my camera on a path on the mountain. Jane Torrance had taken photographs that day, of the girls and their travels, and this is what we found when we developed the film.'

Shuffle-click.

The girls walking in the forest.

Shuffle-click.

The fork in the path.

One of the girls was sitting on the stone – my stone – in the sunlight.

Another girl was pointing to the path that led up the mountain.

Shuffle-click.

Another picture.

Snow on the ground in the forest.

There were gasps all around me in the darkened refectory.

Shuffle-click.

Snow falling from the sky.

Some of the children shuffled uneasily in their seats.

'Yes,' said Miss Simmons. 'It's snow. Snow like we've never experienced at Eventide House. And there's more.'

Shuffle-click.

A picture of an entire valley blanketed in snow. The trees were bare as in the dead of winter. And down there, at the treeline, was a strange cloud of black smoke. It was entirely black with no grey in it at all, and it clung close to the ground as if it was moving over the land rather than moving through the air.

'These are the last images we have been able to recover from the camera. As you can see, there is something down there in the valley. Some kind of dark cloud.'

The slide projector *shuffle-clicked* and *shuffle-clicked* again, and each time the image of the dark cloud came closer, as if it was moving, pulsating, flowing across the ground like an insect with a million tiny legs. A terrible hushed murmur rippled through the refectory, and the children shifted in their seats.

It's death, I thought.

But not the death we've experienced here.

It's something else.

It's worse.

'Can anyone tell me what it is?' said Miss Simmons.

'It's a monster,' said a girl somewhere behind me.

'Yes,' said Miss Simmons. 'It is indeed a monster. We've heard stories about this cloud, some of them going back centuries, but no one has succeeded in capturing it on film before. We have never had proof.'

I stared at the cloud.

It was dark and malevolent; it was cruel and uncaring.

It was hungry; it wanted something from us.

'Lights, please,' said Miss Simmons.

The lights came on and the slide projector was turned off.

Nobody moved. No one was in a hurry to go to bed.

There was a terrible silence in the refectory.

'Mrs Cauke,' said Miss Simmons.

'Thank you,' said Mrs Cauke, and all eyes turned to the

headmistress, who remained seated, off to one side, with a cup of coffee cradled in her hands. She did not speak for a moment: she seemed to be choosing her words carefully.

'The girls are gone,' she said. 'Gone forever, we believe. And this black cloud had something to do with it. We believe it took them. Where it took them we do not know. No one has ever returned from an encounter with the black cloud to tell us what it is and what it means. And I'm afraid that is the limit of our knowledge.

'You may ask questions.'

There were many questions, and no satisfactory answers.

'Where does it come from?'

'Is it alive?'

'How do we stop it?'

'Is it smoke?'

'Is it fire?'

'We don't know,' Mrs Cauke answered to all of them. 'All we know is that the black cloud has never been here at Eventide House. It seems to prefer higher ground where the air is thinner. It seems to prefer the cold. It seems to prefer snow.'

Justin, I thought.

Justin.

He took the path to the right, up the hill, up the mountain – where the air is thinner, where it's colder, where it might even rain, where it might even snow.

'That is all,' said Mrs Cauke. 'Goodnight, children.'

'Goodnight, Mrs Cauke,' said the children.

'Remember,' she said. 'You're safe here.'

Chapter Forty-Five

I went downstairs in the middle of the night without making a sound. I knew my way around now: I knew where everything was, even in pitch darkness; where the floorboards creaked; where I might trip on some loose corner of carpet.

Except . . .

Except there were other people up and about in the night. I could hear voices, and I hid and waited and heard footsteps going past. I went on and when I turned the corner into the library passage, I saw that the door was open and there was a light inside.

I crept into the library and hid behind the bookstacks, and looked.

Mrs Cauke was holding a lantern, standing in front of

the secret door, which was open. She was staring at Ash's hiding place.

There were footsteps and Miss Simmons entered with some papers.

'Here,' she said, as she approached Mrs Cauke. 'I've found her. Aisling Walsh. Due on the fourteenth of last month. But nobody's seen her. I assumed someone on the other side had made a mistake.'

'They don't make mistakes,' said Mrs Cauke. 'She's been here the whole time. She's been hiding from us – in there.'

They both looked at the secret room.

'I didn't even know this place existed,' said Miss Simmons.

'Neither did I,' said Mrs Cauke.

'I'll check the kitchens,' said Miss Simmons.

'Yes,' said Mrs Cauke. 'And then the chapel.'

The chapel! I thought.

'We cannot allow her to disrupt our research,' said Mrs Cauke.

I turned and ran.

Chapter Forty-Six

There was a faint glow coming from inside the well. I leaned over the side and looked down; I could see Ash's lantern far below.

'Ash!' I whispered. 'Ash!'

There was the sound of running water and Ash's face appeared below. She was standing on the jetty at the bottom of the ladder.

'Eleanor,' she said, looking up. 'I've got something amazing to tell you.'

'Tell me later,' I said. 'They're coming.'

'Who's coming?'

'Mrs Cauke and Miss Simmons. They've found your hiding place.'

'Oh,' said Ash.

'They're on their way here right now,' I said.

'I'm coming up,' said Ash. She put a hand on the ladder and started to climb up. Then she slipped, I think – I'm not sure – and the lantern fell from her hand into the black water and went out.

All was darkness down there.

'Ash?' I whispered.

'I'm still here,' she said. 'I'm coming.'

I heard the squeak of her trainers on the rungs below.

'Hurry,' I whispered.

'I am,' she said. I could hear the effort in her voice.

In the faint light that remained I noticed the library key lying on the wall around the well. I looked back at the door to the chapel, and then I pocketed the key.

Ash's face appeared in the pale gloom below. She was out of breath, climbing up. 'I've got something very important to tell you, Eleanor . . . I think I've discovered what's going on here . . .'

'Hurry,' I said.

'I think I've discovered where we are,' she said.

There were footsteps coming along the passage outside the chapel.

'Now,' I said. 'Come on!'

'We're not really here,' said Ash.

The footsteps were right outside the door.

'They're here,' I whispered.

I looked back: the handle in the door turned and I hid between two pews.

The chapel door opened and lantern light fell on the floor, and footsteps came closer. I saw Mrs Cauke walk past, then Miss Simmons.

I raised my head and peered over the top of the pew.

Ash emerged from the well, pulling herself up on to the edge.

Only then did she see Mrs Cauke in front of her.

'Mrs Cauke,' said Ash.

Mrs Cauke nodded. Then she did something I hadn't been expecting.

She put her hand on Ash's chest and pushed.

I saw Ash's mouth go wide in surprise, and then she disappeared. There was a scream, and the scream faded as she fell like a stone, and then there was a splash and Ash was gone, into the river.

No one said anything for a moment.

No one moved.

I had my hand over my mouth; I could barely breathe.

Finally Miss Simmons said, 'Are you sure that was wise?'

'I'm not sure of anything,' said Mrs Cauke.

'Where has she gone do you think?' said Miss Simmons.

'Into darkness and oblivion,' said Mrs Cauke. 'Or somewhere else entirely. I really have no idea. She is no longer our responsibility.'

Mrs Cauke turned and walked away. After a moment Miss Simmons followed.

'We must change the locks,' said Mrs Cauke as they went out.

'We really must,' said Miss Simmons.

I waited for their footsteps to fade away into the night. Then I went to the well and leaned forward over the edge, and looked into the blackness.

'Ash!' I whispered. 'Ash!' No answer.

Nothing down there, only the dark.

I sat on the side of the well and swung my legs over and lowered myself down until my feet found the rungs of the ladder. Then I climbed down into darkness, hand over hand, step after step, until I'd reached the last rung.

'Ash!' I said. 'Ash, where are you?'

No answer.

She was gone – wherever the current had taken her.

The river glittered darkly and all around me there was silence. I listened for the voices I'd heard last night;

I listened for the sounds of Home. I waited, hoping they'd come, but there was only silence and darkness.

'Speak to me,' I said to the cold watery air. 'Speak to me, please.'

No answer.

'Say something,' I said. 'Somebody, please . . . Anyone . . . I don't want to be alone . . .'

Nothing.

This is it, I thought. *This is what being a ghost feels like.*

Like being far from home, and alone, in the middle of the night.

I climbed up and let myself out of the chapel, and crept away, miserable, to bed.

Chapter Forty-Seven

I left as soon as it was light.

I stopped at the refectory only to down a cup of coffee and take some bread rolls for later, and then I set off.

It was cold outside. The sky was brightening in the east but I couldn't see the sun. I walked through the dew on the grass to the treeline and up the path into the woods.

*

It was still cold when I came to the fork in the path.

It had rained in the night, I saw. At least, it had rained up here on the mountain. The earth was dark with the rain and Justin's last message – his warnings to me – had been washed away.

I sat down on the rock and rested. I'd been walking fast;

I could feel the cool of my sweat inside my clothes.

I should have brought some water, I thought.

I looked at the path to the right.

I had nothing to lose.

I am going to follow you, Justin.

I am going to follow you no matter what you say.

I am going to follow you because I have to know.

I got to my feet.

I did what I'd been too scared to do until now.

I set off along the path to the right.

*

I climbed. There was only the path, only the steady rise of the ground beneath my feet. There were no other forks in the path and I had no idea where I would end up.

Gradually the trees thinned out and the land grew rockier. Pockets of snow appeared, shadowed by rocks. I stopped to look back, and saw how high I was and how far I'd come. The sun was high in the morning sky; it felt warm on my face and I could hear the trickle of snowmelt.

There was the land below, and the river.

How beautiful it is, I thought.

This is what I love.

A path. A trail. A forest.

Walking into the future under a warm sun.

It was the sort of landscape I would have invented for myself to live in.

It was the sort of world I'd have created if I'd been God.

I left the path, and found meltwater running quietly over some dark rocks, and I cupped my hands and drank, and drank again, and then I went on.

There was snow on the path now, and before long I saw a trail of footprints.

Justin.

My boots went *crunch-crunch-crunch* in the snow, following Justin's tracks. Then I came to a ridge above a snow-covered valley and I stopped.

I couldn't believe my eyes.

Down there in the valley was my school. *Our school.*

Three buildings of pale-yellow brick standing in a field of snow.

It seemed to have been plucked out of time and space, and simply dropped here. There were no children anywhere, no sign that there was anybody inside the school now. A few windows were broken; it had been left to the elements.

I followed Justin's footprints down into the valley.

The closer I got, the more certain I became that this was our school. I stopped at the steps to the main entrance and listened. All around me was a cold, dead silence. No birds. No wind.

'Hello!' I shouted, and my voice echoed off the mountain.

No answer.

'HELLO!'

Nothing.

'Justin! JUSTIN!'

Chapter Forty-Eight

The main door creaked open and I stepped into the school.

It was like stepping into an alternative reality.

It was as if there had been some kind of emergency – a fire alarm or a bomb threat – and everyone had been told to evacuate now, this instant, and not to come back. There was dust over everything and cobwebs floated in the air. Chairs and tables lay broken, trampled, along the central corridor. Snow lay clustered in little piles where winter gusts had blown it in.

I felt terribly alone.

'Hello?' I said. 'Is there anybody here?'

No answer.

My breath misted in the cold air.

I could see Justin's footprints in the dust on the floor – I recognised the zigzag pattern of his trainers – and I followed him up the stairs and into the classroom at the top of the building where we used to have history and ancient civilisation. It was empty apart from the desks and the chairs, and I went to the window to look out.

Everything was snow; everything was perfect and frozen.

My focus shifted and I saw colours on a wall behind me, reflected in the glass, and I turned. There on the wall was all that remained of our last school project. The project we'd been working on before we died: maps of the world of the ancient Greeks and the underworld, and the rivers of Hades; and drawings of Charon and Cerberus, and Orpheus and Eurydice.

There was the desk where I used to sit. And right behind it was Justin's desk.

There was something on his desk and I went quickly to it.

It was a tape.

A blank tape with Justin's name written on it.

Justin's tape from the Walkman.

I picked it up and the moment I did so, a shadow fell across the room.

I turned and there it was, outside the classroom window.

The black cloud.

It was billowing right in front of me. I stared at it. I couldn't take my eyes off it.

It wasn't just a scary story like all the other scary stories. It was alive. Everything inside it was in motion, pulsating: it billowed this way, it shivered that way, it soared, reaching for something, trying to grasp the air in its hand, and meanwhile it kept coming closer to the window, creeping forward like a giant insect.

Then it was here: it covered the window; the room grew dark.

I knew what had happened to the girls who'd disappeared in the snow; they'd been swallowed by this thing. They'd been eaten and they were gone forever, and I knew then that the cloud was Death and that it was going to get me too, unless I ran . . .

I turned and bolted from the room.

Tendrils of black smoke curled in through the windows in the corridor.

I ran down the stairs and on to the main entrance, where I crashed out through the doors and down the snow-covered steps.

I ran.

I didn't look back.

Chapter Forty-Nine

I ran through the snow until there was no snow beneath my feet, and then I ran on until there was no breath left in my lungs, and only then did I look back, and there was only the forest behind me and no sign of the black cloud.

It hadn't followed me.

It didn't want me yet.

I slowed to a walk and my breath came back, and then I stopped, and I realised I still had Justin's tape in my hand.

I looked back along the path, and I knew what had happened to him. What must have happened to him. He'd come this way; he'd arrived at the school, but he hadn't been warned about the black cloud as I had been. He wouldn't have known to run. He wouldn't have known how hungry it was.

The black cloud had taken him.

He was gone, and suddenly I felt very clearly that I would never see him again.

Tears sprang to my eyes and I couldn't stop them, and I walked slowly back to the fork in the path, the last place I'd seen him. The sun was low in the sky and I heard the dinner bell ringing, far away in the valley, but I didn't move. I didn't care.

I didn't care about anything any more. Justin was gone. I'd never see him again.

I sat down on the rock by the side of the path and let my tears fall to the ground.

It was only when I'd stopped crying that I noticed something written in the bare earth at my feet. Another message scratched in the dust with a stick.

A message from Justin.

The last message.

Listen.

This time there was no mistaking what it meant. I looked from the message on the ground to the tape I held in my hand.

Listen to the tape.

Chapter Fifty

Darkness fell. I remained outside in the cool night air, watching the house, waiting for the others to go to bed. One by one, all the lights in all the windows were extinguished and the house stood in darkness.

No light in the library window tonight.

I went across the grass to the house and silently in through the main door. Then up the stairs to my room, where I retrieved the library key from beneath my pillow, and then back downstairs again, making no sound, stopping every now and then to listen to the sound of the house asleep.

I came to Mrs Cauke's office and put the key in the lock and turned it.

A quiet, satisfying *clunk*.

Books unlock every door.

Books unlock all secrets in the end.

The door opened and I crossed to the desk in the gloom. I sat in Mrs Cauke's chair and opened the drawers in the desk until I found my Walkman. Then I pressed eject and took out the tape with my name on it and replaced it with Justin's.

I hesitated, wondering if what I was about to do was allowed. If it's ever right to listen to someone else's tape. It suddenly seemed private and deeply personal, like I was about to look into his mind. Into his soul.

Listen, he'd written in the dirt.

I put the headphones on and pressed play.

There was a *click*, and the tape turned inside the machine.

Hiss . . .

I didn't know what I expected to hear, what I expected to find out. But I knew what I wanted: what I wanted was to hear his voice one more time.

I wanted it desperately.

'Justin?' I said.

Hiss . . .

'Justin, are you there?'

More *hiss*, and then a *voice*. 'I'm here.'

I gasped.

It was him. His voice.

'Justin!'

'I'm here,' he said. 'Ellie?'

'It's me, I'm here.'

'Where's here?' he said. 'Where are you?'

'I'm at a place called Eventide House,' I said.

'Eventide House?' he said. 'But you can't be.'

'Why not?' I said.

'Because *I'm* at Eventide House,' he said.

For a moment neither of us said anything. I suddenly felt cold all over, as if I was afraid – as if I was afraid without really understanding why.

'I'm at Eventide House,' he said again, quietly.

'But you're not here,' I said. 'I'm here, Justin, and I haven't seen you.'

'I'm here, Ellie,' he said. 'I've been here since the day we parted on the path through the woods. I've been waiting for you.'

I hesitated.

I knew Justin wasn't at Eventide House.

Not *my* Eventide House, anyway.

'What's it like, where you are?' I said. 'Tell me about it. Describe it.'

'There's a river,' said Justin. 'And a valley. The house is in the valley. It's big, like a castle, and it's hundreds and hundreds of years old . . . And when you step inside, there's a mirror in the hall. A great big arched mirror, tall enough for you to stand in front of it and see yourself from head to toe.'

'Yes,' I whispered.

'Does that sound like Eventide House to you?'

'It does,' I said.

'Then one of us is lying,' he said.

'I don't believe that,' I said.

'Neither do I,' he said. 'But maybe one of us is being deceived.'

I had an idea then.

'Meet me,' I said.

'What?'

'If you're here,' I said. 'Meet me.'

'All right,' he said. 'Where?'

'By the mirror in the hall.'

'All right,' he said, and I heard him move. 'I'm on my way.'

I crossed the room and stepped out into the corridor.

All was dark and quiet; no one but me was awake.

'I'm coming,' I whispered. I went along a passage and

turned a corner and went down another passage, and then I was in the hall.

I stopped in front of the great arched mirror.

'Nearly there,' said Justin in my ears. It sounded as if he was coming down the stairs, but there was no one on the stairs above me.

I looked at myself in the mirror.

'I'm here,' I said in a whisper. 'Are you there?'

'I'm here,' he said. 'I'm right here. I'm standing in front of the mirror.'

'I don't see you,' I said. All I saw was myself.

'I don't see you either,' he said.

Neither one of us said anything for a moment. I looked around the hall. All I saw were shadows, and I felt cold again, and frightened, and my eyes fell on the cactus on the small table in the corner at the bottom of the stairs.

'Is there a cactus where you are?' I said.

'A cactus?'

'Yes,' I said. 'On the table in the corner by the stairs.'

'No,' he said. 'No, there's no cactus.'

'There's one here,' I said.

Then Justin said, 'Is it snowing where you are?'

'Snowing?' I said. 'No. Why?'

'It's snowing here,' he said. 'It feels like it's always winter here.'

It's always summer here, I thought, but I didn't say it.

I suddenly felt very sorry for Justin.

'We're in different places,' he said. 'And I don't quite understand why.'

'Neither do I,' I said.

'I've been waiting for you all this time,' he said, 'and you're not coming. You're already here, it's just that *your* here isn't the same as *my* here.'

'Will I see you again?' I said.

'I don't know, Ellie,' he sighed. 'I just don't know.'

'Justin,' I said. 'Please. You said you had a plan. Now come on. You always have a plan. Please. Figure it out.'

'All right, all right,' he said. 'Let me think.'

I looked down at the tape going round inside my Walkman and saw that it was spooling to the end; there was very little time left.

'There is a way,' he said quietly.

'What is it?'

'We go back,' he said. 'Back across the river. Back to the world of the living. Both of us. We meet there.'

'OK,' I said. 'Then what?'

'Then . . . We'll figure out what to do next.'

'Justin . . .'

'Trust me, Ellie,' he said. 'You're going to have to trust me. I promise you everything is going to be all right.'

'I trust you,' I said.

'There's a boat,' he said.

'I know,' I said. 'I know where it is.'

'You'll come?'

'I'll come.'

'Thank you.'

'And you'll be there?'

'I'll be there,' he said. 'Bring the tape with you. My tape, so we can find each other.'

I looked at the Walkman; the tape was almost at an end.

'You promise you'll be there?' I said.

'I'll be waiting for you,' he said. 'Now go back, Ellie. Go back to the world of the living.'

There was a *click*; the tape had stopped. I turned it over and pressed play – but there was nothing on the other side of the tape: no Justin, just silence, and the faraway hiss of the tape running through the machine.

He was gone.

Chapter Fifty-One

I went to bed. I lay there in darkness and finally a sort of sleep engulfed me: a wakeful slumber with dreams that vanished the moment I realised I was dreaming.

I woke to a faint but enveloping sound, and it took me a moment to work out what it was.

Rain.

I hadn't heard rain since I was alive. It was falling softly but steadily, and I got up and pulled the sash window down a crack and sat on the windowsill and felt the cold fresh scent of it on my face.

The wind began to pick up. It strafed leaves from the trees – leaves that were beginning to turn brown; they curled through the air like little flocks of birds.

Some kind of autumn was coming, as surely as the world

turns. Dark clouds held the sky over the river.

A storm was coming.

For half an hour or so, my eyes never left the sky. I don't remember having any conscious thought in all that time. My senses felt open to the elements; I watched nature unfold itself. There was the sense of something electric in the air, something against my skin, something that was going to change things here and in the other world.

CRASH . . .

Lightning, over there in the east.

The rain came at a cold pelt then, battering the window, but there was something else in the sky over there, something moving – a bird perhaps, a high hovering bird – except it lacked a bird's grace.

Except it was *red*.

I leaped forward and raised the window fully open now, and the rain came in with a blast, wetting my face, but I could see.

It was a kite, over there in the sky.

A red kite.

My kite, calling me home.

There was the boat and the river, and here was the rain. The rain would pour into the river, and the river would rise to meet the boat, and the boat would be lifted clear of the mud, and someone like me – a child, by myself – could push it out of the shallows and into the open water where the current would carry me home.

Hold on.

I'm coming.

Chapter Fifty-Two

On my way downstairs I saw Mrs Cauke in the hall below and I froze.

She was counting the umbrellas in the stand by the door.

'You can come down,' she said without looking at me. 'The breakfast things are ready. I'll be going along myself in a moment.'

Murderer, I thought.

Murderer.

I came slowly down the stairs. What daylight there was fell sombre through the windows and the sound of the house was different: everything was muffled, far away. It was like being underwater.

Mrs Cauke drew one of the umbrellas out of the

stand and held it up in the air. 'Funny things, umbrellas. They get carried away by the wind so easily. They seem to be able to cross between the worlds. It pays to keep track of them.'

She dropped the umbrella back into the stand.

'One missing,' she said. She seemed puzzled.

I didn't say anything. I didn't want to say anything to her. Ever.

She became aware of my silence and looked at me closely then. She narrowed her eyes. I could hardly breathe.

Did she know I was there in the chapel that night? Did she know I saw what she did to Ash?

'You're not thinking of leaving us just yet, are you, Eleanor?' she said.

I flinched.

'Surely you're not thinking of moving on to another place?'

I shook my head.

'No,' I said. 'No. I'm staying.'

'Good,' she said. 'It's too soon, Eleanor. We really are doing our best to help you. Everything that can be done is being done.'

Above us the bell rang for breakfast. The children came down slowly, in ones and twos. They were subdued:

worried about the rain; frightened of the storm. I joined them in the refectory, aware of Mrs Cauke's eyes on me.

*

It rained and rained. The children did not venture out. They congregated in the games room where they played table tennis and board games, and a chess match which had long ago been abandoned was eagerly resumed. Some sat in the window seats, their eyes on the world outside, doing nothing, watching the constant motion of water in the air. Others played some kind of cricket with a tennis ball in the long passageway.

Time passed.

I needed more rain. I needed the ground saturated. I needed the river to flood.

I waited and watched the rain come down in droves.

The black umbrellas stood unused in the stand by the front door.

At six o'clock the bell rang for dinner, summoning the children, and for a moment it might have looked as if I was going with them. I got up from where I was sitting by the window in the games room and followed the others into the hall. Then I slipped away upstairs.

I changed into my old clothes in my room – my own

clothes, the clothes I'd died in. Then I came downstairs again. Seeing that there was no one about, I took an umbrella from the box by the door and stepped outside.

Chapter Fifty-Three

The world was a shining surface of water. There was nowhere to walk without getting your feet soaking wet. I stuffed my socks into my trainers and carried them, and went barefoot on the grass.

I didn't look back.

I walked to the fork in the path and on to the stream, and then I followed it down the other side of the mountain. It grew into a river, and the path beside it turned into mud, and I went on; it felt like cold hands around my ankles trying to hold me back.

I waded through shallow water, and then I came to the boat. It was still there, and the river had risen around it.

I threw my trainers into the belly of the boat and placed the open umbrella over them. Then I pulled off the branches that had been put there to hide it.

The boat was turned away from the water, with its nose pointing in towards the land and its stern to the river. I waded through the knee-high swamp and placed my hands on the nose of the boat.

One push and it slid quickly backwards, and stopped. I followed it and put my hands on the nose again, and braced.

Another push and it moved again, and stopped.

The bottom of the boat was stuck in the mud below.

Heave, I thought. *Heave! Heave-ho!*

It was enough. The boat curled silently away from me, out into open water. Then it began to turn like a leaf on the surface of a puddle, and for a moment I thought it was going to drift off without me, so I ran and splashed after it. Mud clung to my feet and cold water circled my thighs, but I made it and grabbed hold of the boat and hurled myself over the side and I was in.

The boat turned in the water and I brought up the oars, but I didn't need to row: the current running back to the world of the living was strong. I used one of the oars to steer, sitting in the prow of the boat, punting us away from the banks.

An hour passed, maybe more, and finally I saw an old

stone archway covered with ivy, and the darkness of the tunnel mouth within.

The water quickened.

Darkness swallowed me up. There was the omnipresent sound of water, and the water was black and the walls of the tunnel were black. There was a rushing sound, growing louder: a gushing, drumming sound, like water pouring over a weir or—

Like a waterfall.

The bottom dropped out of the world.

The boat went over the edge of something, tipping forwards, and I fell. My stomach jumped into my mouth and air rushed past my skin, and I fell.

There seemed to be no end to the falling.

Chapter Fifty-Four

Something happened in the falling.

There was a moment of silence, and I saw a light.

A warm, yellowy light moving towards me.

It came closer and closer, and I saw that it was a lantern.

Someone was walking towards me carrying a lantern.

It was Ash.

She came closer: she came right up to me and held the lantern up to my face, and then she smiled and I knew where she was, where she'd fallen when she was pushed down the well: she'd fallen here, in the darkness between the world of the dead and the world of the living, and it was my job to get her out of here.

'Ash,' I said.

I reached for her hand, and the lantern went out and I was falling again.

Chapter Fifty-Five

On the south bank of the river Thames, in the world of the living, an oar fell from the sky and landed in the soft brown mud at the edge of the water.

The tide was out: far enough out for mudlarks to be about their work, combing the silt and sludge on the banks of the Thames for riches and curios from days gone by. One such mudlark, a teenage boy in a pair of waders that were much too big for him and holding a metal detector, saw the oar fall and impale itself in the mud only a few metres away from him. It stood upright like a spear, and when the boy took a step towards it, the second oar fell from the sky and landed precisely where he'd been standing only a second before. Then the mudlark heard someone spluttering, as if they'd accidentally swallowed a mouthful of water, but when he turned to see who it was, there was no one there.

I lay where I'd fallen on the shore, half in, half out of the water. I was soaked and stunned, but I was breathing. I felt alive. I sat up and coughed up some more river water, and spat it out, and then I looked at the mudlark.

He was looking right through me. He could see the dent I'd made in the mud. The outline of a small person. He couldn't see me.

There was blank confusion written all over his face.

I got to my feet and looked for Ash, expecting to see her lying there in the wash, but there was no sign of her.

Then I saw something else falling out of the sky.

'Look out!' I shouted, and the mudlark frowned and took a step towards me, and stopped. Behind him, the boat came down out of the sky and crash-landed with a *burrumph* sound in the mud, and the mudlark leaped out of his skin.

'My word,' he said to himself. He looked up at the sky, wondering where it had come from and if there was anything else up there that was likely to fall on him.

One last thing fell from the sky: the umbrella.

Floating down gently in the wind. It landed just beside the boat.

Right then it started to rain.

The mudlark walked over, picked up the umbrella and held it over his head. He stood there in the softly falling rain, feeling – I think – lucky to be alive.

Chapter Fifty-Six

I took the tube home, and when I came back up into the London air, the sky had darkened behind me in the east. Commuters marched by, their minds elsewhere, and I walked through it all, unseen, a ghost.

All I could think of was home.

I passed the Traveller's Return on the corner and turned into our road. I saw our house at the end, and my my heart beat faster in my chest.

Home!

I broke into a run. I ran up the steps to the front door.

I pressed the doorbell and buzzed it and buzzed it, and then I reached up and rapped on the door with the little metal knocker.

No answer.

No lights on inside either.

I crouched down and shouted through the letterbox.

'Mum! Dad!'

I couldn't see anyone inside. I stood on the edge of the steps and leaned out and looked in through the living-room window. Everything was the same: our things, our furniture; the same as always.

I cupped my hands around my mouth and shouted through the glass.

'MUM! DAD!'

No one home.

I sat down on the steps and looked across the road at Justin's house. There were lights on in the windows and I could hear the baby, Daniel, crying, and I wondered where Justin was and how long it would take him to get here.

Then I leaned back against the front door and it opened.

Or rather, it swung open and I fell in.

I went inside; the door swung shut behind me and locked with a *clunk*.

'Justin?' I said in the half-light.

No answer.

I stood there listening for a moment.

There was the familiar hum of the old fridge in the kitchen, but nothing else.

I went upstairs to my room. It was the same – except tidier. Everything had been very neatly arranged and put away. It was much tidier than it had ever been when I was alive.

I lay down on my bed and my head on my pillow felt like the most comfortable thing in the universe. It felt like home.

I didn't want to move.

I could stay here, I thought. I could stay here for ever. I could be a comfortable ghost right here, watching all the comings and goings.

Outside the daylight had faded.

The streetlights will come on in a moment, I thought.

There was something on the windowsill next to the old toy boat.

My dad's Walkman and a pair of headphones.

The streetlights came on and in the light that fell through the window I picked up the Walkman and untangled the headphones and put them on. Then I took Justin's tape out of my pocket and put it into the Walkman and pressed play.

There was a *click*.

'Justin?' I said. 'Are you there?'

'I'm here,' he said. It was as if he was in the room with

me, as if he was standing right beside my shoulder, but he wasn't there. I was alone.

'Ellie, where are you?' he said.

'I'm home,' I said.

'Where, precisely?'

'In my house,' I said. 'In my room.'

'OK,' he said. 'Now, I want you to prepare yourself for a shock. Time moves faster here than it does in the other world. And while it may seem like only a few days have passed for you at Eventide House, six months have gone by here.'

Six months.

'Are you sure?' I said.

'I'm sure.'

Time had rolled on without me here. It had left me behind. Everyone I'd known was six months older already.

They would have started to forget me.

Days might go by and they wouldn't even think of me.

'Now,' said Justin. 'I want you to do something for me.'

'What?'

'Go to the window and tell me what you see.'

'All right.'

I climbed on to the bed and sat at the windowsill, looking out.

'Are you there?' said Justin.

'Yes.'

'What do you see?'

Across the way, the lights were on in Justin's house. I could see the whole family going about their daily lives. There was some kind of life in every window and it looked like home, and it looked like *heaven*. There was Ayesha, Justin's younger sister, in the living room playing the piano. And there was Mr Fletcher in the kitchen, leaning over the stove while various pots bubbled around him and the window steamed up. And there was Justin's mum, Laura, in the room at the front upstairs, with Daniel.

'I see everybody,' I said. 'They're all here. It looks . . . wonderful.'

'Yes,' whispered Justin.

'It looks perfect. I can see Ayeesha,' I said. 'She's playing the piano. She's practising . . . wait.'

I leaned forward and opened my window on the early evening light.

'Listen,' I said, and we listened.

We could hear Ayeesha practising; the notes she played

on the piano drifted peaceably out through the half-open window beside her and across the street, and up to where I sat at my window.

'Do you hear it?' I said.

'I hear it,' said Justin.

'What is it?' I said.

'It's *Clair de lune*.'

'It's beautiful,' I said.

'It is.'

'I can see your dad,' I said. 'He's making dinner downstairs in the kitchen.'

'What's he cooking?' said Justin.

'Can't tell,' I said. 'Some kind of stew. Lots of chopped vegetables.'

'Ratatouille,' said Justin. 'Which means it's Thursday.'

'And I see your mum,' I said. 'She's upstairs with Daniel. She's holding him. He's crying. She's trying to calm him.'

Mrs Fletcher was at the window looking out across the road.

Looking at me, I thought.

'She looks tired,' I said.

'I'll bet,' said Justin, and then Mrs Fletcher leaned forward and breathed on the window in front of her, and as her breath steamed up the glass she wrote the letter J in the condensation with her finger, and I saw the baby staring at the J, and he quietened.

'She's thinking about you,' I said.

'How do you know?' he said.

'She just drew the letter J on the window,' I said.

She was talking to the baby now, and I knew what she was saying to him.

'She's telling Daniel all about you, Justin.'

Justin didn't say anything.

'She's telling him how wonderful you are.'

Still Justin was silent.

'She thinks about you all the time,' I said.

I could see it. It was true.

'Every day,' I said.

I could hear Justin sobbing, and then he said, 'Lord, I wish I could see her.'

'You can,' I said. 'You'll see her. You're coming.'

He was silent again.

'Justin . . . you're coming, aren't you?'

He didn't answer for a moment, and then he said, 'I wish, Ellie.'

'Wait,' I said. 'Wait a minute. You said you were coming.'

Justin didn't answer. I could hear him breathing and I could feel myself falling.

Falling through the sky like a kite plummeting down to earth.

He isn't coming.

My eyes felt hot with tears.

'You told me we would find each other here,' I said. 'You told me *we* were coming back. You told me you had a plan.'

'I do have a plan,' he said. 'But not for us. Not for me. For you.'

'Us, Justin. You said *us*.'

'. . . I lied.'

'You lied?' I said. 'Why?'

'Because I had to get you back,' he said.

'What about you?' I said. 'Don't you have to get back too?'

'Some of us can come back, and some of us can't,' he said.

'Why not?'

'Because we can't,' he said. 'Because it's over. But it's different for you. There are still things you have to do in this world. There are still things you need to see.'

'I don't understand, Justin.'

'Six months have passed, Ellie,' said Justin. 'Think about it.'

I turned away from the window.

I went out of the room, across the landing, into the den.

Except the den wasn't the den any more. The den was the nursery. All our things were gone: the desk, all my dad's stuff, all the clutter. The room had been painted a light cream colour, and there was a cot and a deep carpet and some cuddly toys.

My brother, I thought.

My baby brother.

'Is he here?' I said.

'He's arrived in the world, yes,' said Justin. 'You need to go now and meet him. But I want to thank you. For being my eyes. For letting me know my mum and dad and sister and brother are OK.'

'Where is he?' I said. 'Where's my brother?'

'He's at the hospital. They're all at the hospital.'

'Which one?' I said, and he told me. I knew where it was.

'I'm going,' I said.

Chapter Fifty-Seven

I went to the hospital. It was dark now. Ambulances came and went, and I saw patients being stretchered in and others coming out in wheelchairs.

Old people, mostly; old people who had lived long lives.

Then there was me. I only had Justin, and he was a voice.

I went into the brightly lit lobby. There was a reception desk and the entrance to the cafeteria on one side, and there were three big metal-doored lifts.

'Where do I go now?' I said.

'Take the lift to the second floor,' said Justin.

I went over, and the lift doors opened and an orderly came out pushing an old man in a wheelchair. I stepped in and pressed the button and the doors closed.

The lift stopped with a *ping*. I stepped out and saw where we were. The maternity ward.

'Go left,' said Justin, and I went left along the corridor. I could hear babies crying.

'Left again,' said Justin. 'Here.'

I stopped. There was a set of double doors – swing doors – in front of me.

'Go in,' said Justin.

I put a hand on one of the doors and pushed, and I went in.

It was a large ward with twelve beds along the walls, and it was full of new mums and new people, sleeping, crying, resting and feeding.

'There's your mum,' said Justin, and I saw her lying on her side in the second-to-last bed, fast asleep. She was wearing a plain hospital smock and beside her bed was a crib, and in the crib was my brother.

I came closer, and looked at my brother. He was awake, his eyes open, looking quietly up at the light shapes in the air above him.

One of those shapes was me.

'He's beautiful,' I said.

'Yes,' said Justin.

I slipped off the headphones.

I leaned forward and stared at the baby. There was a wristband and a name.

Jack.

My brother.

Six months have passed and the world has been made anew.

This is a new beginning, I told myself, for my parents. They couldn't give up, or give in. They had no choice. A whole new person was on his way into their world.

Jack seemed to be looking right at me, although I know new babies don't actually see very much; they see light and shadow, and some big patches of colours.

I reached for his tiny pink hand and held it.

And then something happened.

Jack curled his hand around my finger and squeezed.

I couldn't *breathe.*

I couldn't *think.*

He kept squeezing. He knew I was there.

'I've wanted to meet you all this time,' I said.

Jack squeezed my finger as if to say, *Here I am.*

'I love you,' I said.

Another squeeze. *I know.*

'I envy you,' I said. 'You've got the *best* parents.'

Another squeeze.

'You're going to have a wonderful life,' I said. 'I just wish I could be there to see it . . . I just wish I could hold you.'

I heard a sigh, and saw that my mother had opened her eyes. She shifted herself in the bed and sat up. She was exhausted but she was glowing too. Glowing with an inner light.

Jack let go of my finger and gave a cry, and Mum reached into the crib and picked him up – he was just a little bundle really. She brought him to her on the bed and opened her shirt, and very quickly he started feeding.

'I love you, Mum,' I said, but she didn't hear me and for a moment I just watched her with Jack, feeding him, and I thought – *this is it*.

This is everything.

I pulled the headphones up to my ears. 'Justin?' I said.

'Yes?' he said.

'Where's my dad?'

'He's on his way up in the lift,' he said.

Chapter Fifty-Eight

The lift doors opened and there was my dad – looking sadder than I'd ever seen him look.

He'd lost me, and my heart ached for him.

I wanted to say, 'Sorry.' I wanted to say, 'I'm here.'

His eyes were fixed on the floor ahead of him. He wouldn't have seen me even if I'd been there.

He walked past me to a vending machine and fumbled in his pockets for some change. He pressed a button and a chocolate bar dropped with a *thwump*, and he took it out and unwrapped it and ate it all in one go.

My reflection looked back at him from the glass of the vending machine, but he didn't see me; he didn't know I was there. He didn't sense anything, and somehow that just made me feel sadder.

He turned towards the ward where Mum and Jack were, but when he reached the swing doors he didn't go in. He put his hand on the door and held it there for a moment. Then he changed his mind.

He walked back along the corridor, and I followed. His face was set like stone; his eyes were fixed, unblinking. He went through another door and climbed the stairs, and I followed. Up and up he went, and at the top, on the seventh floor, he stopped to catch his breath, looking out of the window at the city at night, at the river Thames twinkling blackly far below.

I stood beside him and looked at our reflections in the glass.

We were alone. Below us doors opened and closed, and footsteps came and went, but no one disturbed us.

'I miss you,' he said. 'I miss you, Ellie.'

He was talking to me.

It's something he does, I thought, *when he's alone*.

To keep the connection alive. To keep me alive.

I thought about the voices I'd heard at the bottom of the well.

And then I thought about love.

Love.

We talk to the people we love when they're gone.

That's why I talked to Grandma after she'd gone.

That's why Dad was talking to me.

'I know you're not here,' he said.

I'm here.

'I know you can't hear me.'

I can hear you.

'There's Jack,' he said. 'And I love Jack. And I love your mum. Jack's going to have the best life any boy could have. I'll make sure of that. But that doesn't mean I won't miss you every single day of my life.'

I felt hot tears in my eyes, and I put my arms around him and hugged him, knowing he wouldn't feel a thing, and I saw tears in his eyes too, shining there in our reflections above the city.

Then I let him go.

He wiped his eyes and took a deep breath, and then he went through the door to the seventh floor, and I went with him.

Chapter Fifty-Nine

There was nobody at the nurses' station and the corridor was quiet.

Too quiet – it felt like a ghost ward.

I followed my dad to the counter and we waited.

There was an old paperback on the shelf below – something one of the nurses on the night shift was reading, I think. Dad reached over and turned the cover towards us and I saw that it was the Shakespeare play, *A Midsummer Night's Dream*.

The hairs on the back of my neck stood up.

'Justin,' I said.

'Yes,' he answered.

'Where are we?'

'You're home,' he said.

'What do you mean?'

'Look.'

There was the sound of footsteps and I saw a nurse walking down the corridor towards us carrying some papers. As she came closer I thought I recognised her from somewhere. Then my dad waved to her and she waved back, and that's when I realised who she was.

I knew her.

It was Miss Simmons, the drama teacher from Eventide House.

'Justin,' I said.

'Yes.'

'That's . . . that's one of the teachers from Eventide House.'

'Yes,' said Justin.

'What's she doing here?' I said. 'In this world.'

'She's alive,' said Justin. 'She lives here. She works here.'

'Hi, Rachel' said my dad as she arrived at the nurses' station.

'Good evening, Mr Newton,' she said. Her eyes passed briefly over me, or through me. She sat down and logged in to the computer in front of her.

'She doesn't see me, does she?' I said.

'No,' said Justin. 'She can't.'

I looked at her blue uniform and her name on her badge. Rachel.

'How is she?' said my dad.

How is who? I wondered.

'She's sleeping,' said Rachel.

Who's sleeping?

Rachel consulted the computer screen in front of her. 'No changes noted today that I can see,' she said.

'Thanks,' said my dad. He tapped his fingers lightly on the counter. 'I think I'll go and say hello anyway.'

'Please do,' said Rachel and she glanced at her watch. 'I was just about to make some coffee. Can I get you one?'

'That would be lovely, thanks,' said my dad.

'See you in a mo.' Rachel went through a doorway at the back, and my dad put some anti-bac on his hands and then he went down the corridor and disappeared through a set of swing doors. There was a glimpse of a ward beyond with some patients in beds, and the doors swung shut behind him.

I didn't follow him. I had a bad feeling right down in the pit of my stomach. I had an awful, awful feeling. It felt like cold hands reaching through my skin and grabbing hold of my insides.

'Justin?' I said.

'I'm here,' he said.

'What's in there?' I said. 'What's through those doors?'

There was a pause, and then he said, 'You know what's in there, Ellie.'

'No,' I said, 'I don't. I-I don't know.'

'Go in,' he said.

'No,' I said. 'I don't think so. I'm not going in.'

'You must.'

'But I'm scared,' I said.

'Don't be,' he said. 'Trust me.'

Trust me.

'I do,' I said.

'All that's waiting for you through those doors is love,' he said.

I put my hand on the door and went through.

Chapter Sixty

It was an L-shaped ward with six beds right in front of me.
There was a patient in each bed, surrounded by medical
machines. There were heart rate monitors and drips and
machines that beeped quietly, and there was the *hiss* of
breathing machines pushing air into the lungs of some of
the patients who lay there sleeping.

I looked at the patient in the nearest bed, and I knew
her. I knew her in the same way that I knew Rachel:
I knew her from Eventide House: it was Emma, the girl I'd
met on the first day in the other world, the girl who'd been
electrocuted. She was pale and a light sweat lay
on her brow. There was a drip with some clear liquid going
down a tube into her arm, and there were sensors taped to
her skin, and a white plastic tube up her nose

was helping her to breathe.

I stood there and watched her chest rise and fall, and rise.

She was here.

She was alive.

I walked to the next bed and there was Richard, the boy I'd met in the other world, the one who'd been hit by a car. He lay in an uncomfortable position, as if his spine was twisted. He wasn't breathing by himself: a machine was breathing for him. I could see two small pumps inside the machine inflating and deflating, pushing air into his lungs.

But he was here. He was alive.

I went on. There were other children here, and they were all asleep. Reminders of their waking lives had been placed by their beds: pictures of the people who loved them and prayed for them, piles of beloved books, worn out stuffed animals, keepsakes.

Each bed was a sea of 'get well soon' cards.

I knew all the children here: I'd seen them all at Eventide House. I'd seen them on the playing fields or at breakfast in the refectory, or simply passed them in the hall.

'What is this place?' I said.

'This is a place for sleepers,' said Justin. 'A place for dreamers. And this is also where I leave you. I have to go now, Ellie. We're out of time.'

'Wait,' I said. 'Justin, wait.'

'I've guided you this far,' he said. 'I brought you back for this.'

'Wait,' I said. 'What do you mean?'

'I wish I could see what you're going to see,' he said. 'But I can't.'

'Stay, Justin. Stay.' I pleaded.

'I wish I could see you.'

'Wait . . .' I said.

There was a moment of silence, and then he said, 'Bye, Ellie.'

There was a *click*. I looked at the Walkman: the tape had stopped. I took it out to turn it over, but as I did so the tape spooled out of the cassette, twisting and unravelling, a black snake falling over itself, and then it just sat there, tangled in my hands.

'Goodbye, Justin,' I whispered.

I let the headphones hang round my neck.

I looked at the children.

This is the coma ward, I thought.

They may look like they're asleep but this isn't any

239

ordinary sleep. They're deeper than that, deep down, deeper than sleep. Nothing can wake them. No sound or storm will open their eyes. They might be like this for a week, a month, years . . .

I heard footsteps. Rachel – the nurse, Rachel Simmons – passed me with a cup of coffee and disappeared round the corner of the 'L'.

I followed her.

There were six more beds here, six more patients. I saw my dad sitting by a bed at the far end of the ward; Rachel handed him his cup of coffee.

'Here you go,' she said. 'I'll be at the nurses' station if you need anything.'

'Thanks, Rachel,' said my dad.

I was standing beside one of the beds and when I looked at the patient who lay sleeping there I screamed inside.

It was Ash.

She was alive.

Barely.

She looked pale and uncomfortable. Her dark hair lay damp and flat against her skull. She looked thin and her skin was yellowy, and there was a plastic tube up her nose helping her breathe.

'Oh, Ash,' I said. 'Ash, I'm so sorry.'

There were piles of books on her bedside table, I saw.

Ash's books. Her favourites.

Brought here by people who loved her, to keep her company.

The night library.

I looked at Ash, and her words from the last night in the chapel came back to me.

I think I've discovered what's really going on here. I think I've discovered where we are. We're not really here.

I looked at the other children, and I knew where they were. They were in the other world. They were at Eventide House. They were dreaming of Eventide House.

There was the sound of a baby crying, and I looked at my dad. He was playing a video on his phone, a video of Jack, crying. But he wasn't playing it for himself. He was playing it for the girl in the bed he was sitting beside.

'Listen,' I heard him say. 'That's your brother.'

Something inside me twisted and turned and curled up.

I could see the girl in the bed over there.

I could see her, but I didn't believe it.

I took a step, and my legs gave way and I sank to the floor. I reached out and grabbed the rail at the end of Ash's bed like I was lost at sea and the bed was a raft I was clinging to by my fingers.

I couldn't get up. My legs felt like stone. My arms felt like air.

All I could do was breathe.

My Dad stayed where he was, sitting beside the girl in the bed, a girl who was being kept alive by machines.

A machine to measure her heartbeat.

A machine to measure how much oxygen there was in her blood.

A drip to put fluids into her veins.

Jack was crying on the video, in her ears and mine.

I knew who she was.

She was the girl who looked like me.

Chapter Sixty-One

I pulled myself to my feet. I felt like I would fall at any moment, but I had to go over there. I had to see for myself. I took a step, then another, then one more, then I was there. I stared at the girl who looked like me. I stared at me.

She was sleeping. She looked peaceful. Not *at peace*, but peaceful. There was even the trace of a smile on her face: the smile of someone who has closed her eyes and is feeling warm sunshine on her face. It was as if she was happy to lie here for now, as if she had all the time in the world, as if she was stretched out in the back of a boat on a river in summer.

She was alive. She was hanging in there with a little help from medical technology. Her heart was beating by itself and she was breathing by herself, it seemed, but everything else was being done for her.

She was wearing my grandmother's watch on her wrist.

My red kite hung suspended in the air above her bed.

The books I'd read over and over again sat in a pile on her bedside table.

There was a sea of cards there, wishing her well, and pictures too: pictures of Jack and Mum and Dad, and my cousins and Grandma.

All these things were here in case she opened her eyes. So she'd see them even if it was the middle of the night, even if there was no one there just then. So she'd see them and she'd know people loved her and wanted her to come home.

But she's me, isn't she?

She is me.

Which means . . .

Which can only mean one thing . . .

It means . . .

Chapter Sixty-Two

I'm alive.

That's such an amazing thing to say that I think I'm going to say it twice.

I'm alive.

I've been alive all this time.

I've been here all along, in this hospital. I didn't drown; I survived somehow, and since then I've been asleep. I've been in the deepest sleep you could ever possibly imagine, and I've been dreaming. I've dreamed long and hard, trying to make sense of what was happening to me.

You will recall I have what is known as an overactive imagination.

I dreamed of a river and a boatman and three dogs, and I dreamed of a great old house where there were others like me. I made it all up. I told myself a story to explain the world to me, and the story was all the time I'd spent at Eventide House.

There was no river, no boat, no dogs, no house. There had never been any of those things. I heard Grandma's watch ticking because my dad had put it on my wrist, here in the hospital, to comfort me. I heard the music I loved over there because they played the music I loved to me here, hoping to draw me out of my sleep. I saw the red kite in the air over there because they hung the red kite above my bed here to try to pull me back to the world of the wide awake.

I'm alive.

That's why Justin sent me back here. That's why he made me cross the river.

Because he knew I was still here.

Because he knew I didn't belong in the world of the dead. Not yet.

Now, the question is: how to wake up?

Chapter Sixty-Three

There wasn't any coffee on the other side of the river either. The coffee was here, in a cup in my dad's hands. I could smell it from where I lay in my hospital bed.

My dad finished his coffee now.

'I'm going now,' he said to the girl who looked like me – to the girl who was me. 'Going to see your mum and Jack. I'll be back in the morning with another video.'

He got to his feet and leaned over the bed and kissed me on the forehead.

'Goodnight, Princess,' he said.

Princess.

Something stirred in my memory.

My dad walked away and disappeared around the corner of the 'L'.

For a moment I was alone in the ward.

Alone with myself.

I took a step closer to the girl who looked like me.

'Wake up,' I said.

'Ellie.'

'Please wake up.'

I heard footsteps, *clacking* closer, and I turned expecting to see Rachel come around the corner, but it wasn't her.

It was Mrs Cauke.

She didn't see me – at least, I don't think she saw me. She came straight towards me and stopped beside the bed. Then she took hold of the girl-who-looked-like-me's wrist and looked at her watch and began counting silently to herself.

She was taking my pulse the old-fashioned way.

As she had done in the night at Eventide House.

I looked at her white coat and at her name tag.

Doctor Cauke.

Dr Shelagh Cauke.

She was real; I hadn't made her up. I'd been aware of her somehow in the deepest darkest point of my sleep. Just as I'd been aware of Ash and Rachel and the others.

Dr Cauke stopped counting and let go of my wrist. She picked up the chart at the end of my bed and wrote something down on it.

'Help me,' I said, and Dr Cauke turned to look at me with unseeing eyes. I saw that the darkness she'd carried with her at Eventide House was gone. It had been replaced by a calling. A calling to save lives.

'Help me wake up,' I said.

Dr Cauke shivered. A chill had crept up her spine, and she put the chart back and looked closely at the girl in the bed.

'You can do this,' she whispered.

You can do this. But how?

There was a familiar *thump-buddump-buddump*.

I turned and saw that a pile of books had fallen off Ash's bedside table, and in that instant I knew what I had to do. I thought about my dad calling me 'Princess' and the kiss he'd placed on my forehead, and I thought about Ash.

Ash, *sleeping*.

Chapter Sixty-Four

I stood beside Ash's bed.

I remembered the promises we'd made to each other.

I give you permission to kiss me.

On the lips.

In case that's the one thing that's going to wake me up.

'Here goes,' I said.

I brought my face close to hers.

'With this kiss, I thee wake,' I whispered.

I kissed her full on the lips and felt her warmth, and when I drew back, her eyes were open, green and unfocused, and then her dark pupils zeroed in on my face and she saw me, and the world seemed to turn upside down and suddenly I was in bed on the other side of the room, and my eyes were closed and the ward was dark.

I was back in my own body.

I lay there in the lovely dark.

There was a ticking sound somewhere nearby, and I fell asleep.

*

I was in the sky. The wind buffeted me this way and that. I looked down and there was the little patch of London where I lived, twenty or thirty metres below. There was our road: I could see our house, I could see Justin's house, and there was the green of the rec, and there was someone down there flying a kite, and it was the girl who looked like me.

The kite line came up from the spool in her hands, up into the air, all the way up here where I saw that it was tied around my ankle.

Am I a kite?

There was a fleeting shadow and a gust of wind, and I looked and saw that Justin was up in the air with me. He had his arms out; he looked like a superhero except he wasn't wearing a costume or a cape or a mask or anything like that; he just looked like himself.

'We're kites!' I shouted to him above the wind.

'I know!' he shouted back.

I am a kite, I said to myself.

251

I am a kite.

I am spirit.

Justin shouted something else but I didn't catch it. He sounded far away from me; the wind was raging all around us.

'What?' I said.

He cupped his hands around his mouth and shouted, 'I said, we must be in your imagination!'

'How do you know?' I shouted back.

'Think about it!' he shouted. 'That's where all the stories meet! In your imagination!'

'But why mine?' I shouted. 'Why can't we be in your imagination?'

'Because I don't think I'm here!' shouted Justin.

'What do you mean you're not here! I can see you!'

'Look down!'

I looked down – and he was right. There was no one flying him. There was no Justin-on-the-ground keeping Justin-in-the-air tethered to the earth. There was just the girl who looked like me down there, and she was gently but firmly pulling me back down to earth.

'I'm gonna fly now!' Justin shouted. 'I'm going!'

'Goodbye, Justin!' I shouted back to him.

My tears were falling down to earth.

'Bye, Ellie!' he shouted.

The sky behind him was a sea of white clouds.

'Fly, Justin!' I shouted. 'Fly!'

Fly!

And he flew, arms out, superhero-style, zooming up and away from me, looping through the sky back towards me – and passing me one more time in one more dream . . .

*

Daylight, and there was something hovering above my head.

A kite.

A red kite.

My kite.

I blinked, and looked at the window next to the hospital bed and saw that the blinds had been opened, and the glass was dusty and there was weak sunlight outside.

It was morning, and I knew where I was. I was in London and I was alive. I knew what had happened to me. Everything hurt, but I turned my head and looked across the ward.

Ash was lying on her side, her eyes open, looking at me.

I tried to say something but no sound came out of

my mouth. I swallowed and there was a pain in my throat, and I tried again.

'Are we awake?' I said.

My voice was weak and whispery from lack of use.

Ash nodded.

'We woke each other up,' I croaked.

'Yes,' said Ash, weakly.

'. . . How?' I said.

Ash thought about it for a moment and said simply, 'Stories.'

Yes.

'We told each other a story,' she said. 'We left a trail of breadcrumbs . . .'

'Books,' I said.

Books open all doors.

Books unlock all secrets.

Books open all eyes in the end.

I tried to smile, but my face wasn't working properly. I tried to move, but my body wasn't working properly either. Everything hurt, and I tried again and everything hurt even worse than before, but I managed to get my hand to the little buzzer that lay beside me on the bedclothes, and I looked at my wrist, the wrist with my grandmother's watch on it, and I pressed the buzzer to call the nurses. It didn't make any sound in here, but I knew that out there, at the nurses' station, the buzzer was making a quiet urgent noise and someone would come.

Footsteps.

Someone was coming around the corner of the L. Someone would see we were awake.

Chapter Sixty-Five

It was warm in the car coming back from the hospital. It was dark but the streets were clear with a soft rain falling on everything, and I felt calm.

I sat in the front with Dad and rested my head against the window.

Jack was asleep in the back with Mum; they'd been home for months but they'd all come to the hospital to bring me home.

In the meantime I'd been in physio with Ash, learning to walk again.

Baby steps. Getting stronger every day.

We didn't talk in the car: there were too many things to say and nobody knew where to begin anyway. All that would come later. We had survived, all of us; we had all the time in the world now. It was the beginning.

I was going home.

We passed the Traveller's Return on the corner and turned into our road. The pub was open and full of warmth and light and music, and I was glad.

We pulled up in front of our house.

'Do you need some help?' said my dad.

'No,' I said. 'I can do it.'

Dr Cauke called us her little miracles. Waking up from a long coma is rare, she said; recovering so quickly is rarer still. She couldn't really explain it, she said.

'All I can think,' she said, 'is that somebody up there likes you.'

Yes, I thought. *And I know who.*

I opened the car door and reached for the crutches the hospital had given me to help me get around. Then I planted them in the gutter. I took a deep breath and pushed, and lifted myself on to the pavement. I steadied myself, closed the car door behind me and went up the steps to the house.

Behind me Dad was getting Jack out of the car in the car seat.

'Careful,' said Mum.

'I am being careful,' said Dad gently.

I put my key in the lock and went inside. I put the crutches aside and went on by myself, hand over hand along the wall. I came to the bottom of the stairs and took hold of the banister and pulled myself up and up and up until I was on the landing.

Downstairs, Jack cried.

'He wants feeding,' said Mum, and he quietened then.

I stood in the doorway to my room.

I thought I could see a figure inside, a boy in shadow sitting on my bed, and a dog, a sleek black beautiful dog sitting proudly on the windowsill, and two more dogs curled up asleep on either side of the boy.

The boy had his hands over his eyes.

I turned on the light and the boy and the dogs were gone, and there was only the sound of Grandma's watch on my wrist, ticking quietly.

The sound I love.

The sound that reminds me I'm alive.

Chapter Sixty-Six

Justin is dead; he drowned when the mosaic flooded. I would have drowned too if Justin hadn't kept pushing me on towards the way out. Then someone else dragged me up the steps clear of the water, and gave me the kiss of life and kept the blood flowing around my body with sheer brute physical force. The paramedics restarted my heart with a defibrillator and while I remained unconscious, my heart was beating by itself and my lungs started drawing in air by themselves, and I was alive.

I was alive, and Justin was not, and I owed him everything.

*

There is the story of Orpheus, and there's the story of Justin Fletcher. There's the rock star and the schoolboy, the 'hero' and an ordinary boy.

There's the promise Justin made to the gods of the underworld, a promise the gods expected him, like Orpheus, to break. He promised not to look at the people he loved in the world: his mother, father, sister, brother, me. He promised not to look, only to guide my spirit back to where I lay sleeping.

To give me back to life.

*

In the winter when it snowed I walked to his grave and stood there, staring at the stone. I'd prepared a speech for this occasion, but when it came to it, my words seemed small and inadequate. The stone above where his ashes lay in darkness was too real, too physical. It was right there in front of me and all I could do was breathe.

There was no message from him written in the snow, either.

A stick.

I went looking for a stick and found one at the edge of the woods, and came back and wrote THANK YOU in the snow.

He'll see it.

I know he'll see it.

Chapter Sixty-Seven

One day in spring I woke from a deep, dark slumber that was so restful and restorative it felt as if the world had stopped turning. It was Saturday: Mum and Dad were out doing the weekly shop. They'd taken Jack with them; I was alone in the house.

It was raining.

I got a cup of tea and brought it upstairs and sat at the window. I had a book open in my hands, a version of the Grimm Tales I'd borrowed from the library, and when I looked up from my book, there was Grandma coming along the street: a thin woman in a grey coat, holding a black umbrella, walking briskly towards our house. She came up the steps, glanced at her watch and rang the doorbell.

I ran downstairs and opened the door. A gust of wind raced in carrying some rain with it, and Grandma shook her umbrella and stepped inside.

For a moment neither of us said anything.

Grandma looked at me and drank me in with her eyes.

'I'm glad to see you, my dear,' she said. 'But we don't have much time.'

She looked at her watch.

Her watch on *her* wrist.

'Now,' she said. 'Are you alive?'

'Yes,' I said. 'But you're not. You're—'

'Dead,' she said. 'Yes. I know.'

'What do you want?'

'I have been in Erebus,' said my grandma. 'A place of darkness between Earth and Hades. I have lingered there . . . Sometimes I think we've all been in Erebus these past few years and are only now returning to the light . . . And now that you're back, what are you planning to do? What are you going to be when you grow up?'

'A teacher,' I said. 'Like you.'

'Oh, Eleanor,' she said, a little disappointed with me as always. 'You don't have to do anything or be anything just to please me. Your life is yours. You've got to go your own way. You've got to make it – all this – worth it. Now tell me truthfully, what is it you want to be?'

'A doctor.'

Grandmother nodded and smiled. 'Good. Because you're going to be busy, I'm afraid.'

I nodded.

'My dear,' she said. 'I'm so proud of the young woman you're becoming.'

Tears filled my eyes and I remembered what it was I had to say to her. What I hadn't had a chance to say the last time we met, and before that when she was alone in the hospital in the first wave of the pandemic.

'I love you,' I said.

'I love you too,' she said and we hugged there in the hall, and I remembered the smell of her from all those years ago, and a silence descended and I realised that it had stopped raining. Grandma let me go.

'Goodbye, my dear,' she said.

The sky had brightened, and sunlight fell warmly through the door when she stepped outside, and there was birdsong, and she departed.

Acknowledgements

Thanks are due in the first instance to the archaeologists who uncovered the Orpheus mosaic at Littlecote House in the late 1970s, not far from where I grew up. It became a favourite destination for many long walks, and I've always wanted to write about it.

To Caroline Ambrose, Lauren Gardner and Anne McNeil, thank you for everything (once again). To Justine Smith, my agent this year, thank you for your unstinting support. To Lucy Clayton, Kristina Hill, Ruth Girmatsion and Tracy Phillips at Hodder, thank you so much for everything that you do.

To Jenna Mackintosh, my editor, thank you for your patience and careful notes. You helped steer a new course for this book when I was uncertain of everything, and I look forward to working with you on many books to come.

To Izzy Burton, thank you for your wonderful cover art!

To Aaron Hicklin, Matthew Kalil, Ilya Marritz, Hilary Hicklin and Michael Mann, thank you for cheering me on this past year. Thanks also to so many old friends in Liverpool and elsewhere who read the book and reached out to me; it means the world to me.

To Union Square and Sayzansha, thank you for making my dreams come true!

To Ulrica, Kay and Harry, thank you for the happiness you bring into my life every day. I love you all, and I'm grateful for every moment we share.